MUSIC FROM THE EVENING OF THE WORLD

Other books by Michael Brownstein:

Highway to the Sky
Brainstorms
Strange Days Ahead
Oracle Night
When Nobody's Looking
Country Cousins

MUSIC FROM
THE EVENING
OF THE WORLD

MICHAEL
BROWNSTEIN

SUN & MOON PRESS
Los Angeles

Cover: *Study for Recurring Triangle,* by Ross Bleckner.
Acknowledgements: "Ronald Colman" and "The U.P.S. Man" first appeared in *The New Yorker*; "Out West and Back East" and "Lorenzo's Collection" in *The Paris Review*; and "Breakdown on Broadway" in *Fiction*.
This book was made possible through a matching grant from the National Endowment for the Arts and contributions to The Contemporary Arts Educational Project, Inc.

Library of Congress Cataloging in Publication

Brownstein, Michael

New American Fiction Series: 17

ISBN: 1-55713-036-1
ISBN: 1-55713-038-8 [paper]
ISBN: 1-55713-037-X [limited, signed]

FIRST EDITION
10   9   8   7   6   5   4   3   2   1

for REBECCA

CONTENTS

Cathy Is Sailing

Cathy Houghton lived alone in Boulder, Colorado. Years before, growing up as an only child in New England, she used to pretend her parents fit inside an invisible dollhouse. Only then did she feel comfortable with them, only then could she control them. She would dress them, feed them, and put them to bed while, unknowingly, they carried on with their lives. Cathy had transformed her parents into playmates, and they shared a secret life with her until she reached adolescence. Then the dollhouse vanished. By the time she was an adult, Cathy had forgotten about all of this. She had gone to Boston University, majoring in computer arts, and then had moved to Colorado.

Eddie Mayes was a lean, balding, transplanted Virginian in his late thirties, who had attracted Cathy with his relaxed, easy-going manner. Eddie had lived in Boulder for eight years, and owned a business selling solar energy equipment which was located just next door to the downtown bar where they first met. Even though he immediately complained about how slow business was because of the intense competition, he didn't take himself too seriously. He had a curious way of regarding her with a look of mischievous complicity, as if they shared some secret.

"You're the first person I've talked to in months who isn't either buying solar or selling it," he moaned good-naturedly, flashing a self-deprecating smile. "I don't know if I remember how to talk about anything else. Unless you're interested in Uncle Sam's rebate on first-time installations, we may just sit here forever without saying another word."

Cathy decided to take what he said literally.

"Maybe people have the feeling you wouldn't know about anything else. Maybe you have a *need* to look solar, Eddie," she replied soberly. "A need you can't control."

He laughed nervously.

"See, what did I tell you?" he remarked, at a loss as to how to proceed. In order to recover his masculine edge he tried an offhand rejoinder designed to reveal a racy, checkered past, but the challenging tone of her voice had brought him up short, after all. Her clear blue eyes stared at him with a stubborn sadness, as if she knew Eddie was going to disappoint her, and her odd intensity seemed out of place to him in the noisy bar. At a loss for words, he smiled and shrugged, and Cathy liked that. She felt comfortable with his lack of defensiveness.

They dated for six weeks, and had slept together several times, before the night Cathy learned that Eddie was married, that he was in the process of divorcing his wife, that he had two children aged nine and six, and that his wife and he were taking each other to court in order to resolve what share of the business belonged to her. Meanwhile, his wife retained custody of the two boys and was living in their ranch home in North Boulder, while it was Eddie who had to come up with the monthly child support payments.

"The store's barely making money now, anyway," he said ruefully. "Whatever you do, Cathy honey, don't *ever* get married."

Cathy was shocked he had kept this information from her for so long. She felt as if, rather than growing closer to him, she had been playing poker with him all this time. After seeing a movie that night, they had returned to his condominium to find the place trashed. Although she assumed he had been burglarized, Eddie was quite certain something else had happened. Embarrassed and despondent, he soon revealed everything to her.

"I just plain didn't know how to tell you," he said, "so I kept quiet about it. . . . Jessica's such a stranger to me now, it's as if we never could have been married, as if the last ten years never existed. It's spooky."

He was convinced that, earlier that evening, his wife had broken into his place. Among other things, she had managed to let out all the water from his newly installed hot tub, which stood in the solarium through an open doorway. A steaming puddle covered the floor of the living room. Under the dim, indirect lighting, this gave the showy condominium, with its exposed beams and spiral staircase, a desolate, lurid appearance. Various soaked belongings lay scattered around in disarray, and Cathy helped him sort through the mess.

Later, Eddie announced that he didn't think he could spend the night there, so, for the first time since they had met, she took him back to her own apartment. Over the years, Cathy had become very protective of her space. She felt increasingly uncomfortable allowing anyone else inside it. It was her refuge. When she had first moved to Boulder, she could have rented an unfurnished apartment, but the fact that none of the furniture here belonged to her increased her sense of independence. Furniture was unimportant. As far as personal possessions were concerned, she had placed, here and there, little objects and pictures charged with a special significance. They provided a context in which to dream, and were all that mattered to her.

Cathy thought of the apartment as a cave she had happened upon, and which she now inhabited until such a time as she might have to give it up. Consequently, she didn't mind the rather tacky, cracked black leatherette sofa in the living room, or the stained orange carpet, or unmatched vinyl chairs around the flower-patterned formica kitchen table. Eddie, however, after quickly getting drunk, chose to make disparaging comments about the decor in a sour voice she'd never heard him use before.

"This place reminds me of a motel room—can't you afford some decent furniture? With the salary you're earning, you could move outta here and put down a deposit on a new condo. Maybe there's still a membership available out where I live. We'd be neighbors. Then, at least, I wouldn't have to knock before coming over to borrow a cup of sugar, right? I could just walk right in. . . . Knocking's such a damn bore,'' he added wearily.

The cheap rental furniture upset him, he said, because it reminded him of the chaotic scene they had just left at his place. When he suddenly confessed that he missed his two boys, Cathy knew she wasn't going to see him again. She no longer wanted to sleep with him but did so anyway, one last time, because he was drunk and unhappy and because he insisted. While he made love to her, she looked around her apartment apprehensively, as if it might respond to the violation it was witnessing by withholding its favors in the future, and she swore Eddie Mayes would be the last person she ever allowed inside it. He had turned out to be like the other men she had dated, unable to shed the accumulated pressures of daily life, sentimental and manipulative. Before too long, no matter what they were like otherwise, she would return with a sigh of relief to the sanctuary of her apartment, regardless of how keen they were to continue seeing her.

And, in fact, even if on the surface her friendships with the half-dozen women with whom she was close were different, they too proved unsatisfactory. When she was honest with herself, Cathy had to admit that she was involved with them more out of loneliness than from real affection for them. She had difficulty keeping them as friends because these women, too, never lived up to her expectations. She wanted more from women than from the men she picked up in bars, and yet their involvement with life always ended up disappointing her, it was so predictably schematic. For one thing, almost without exception—and whether or not they were bitter about it—they expected no more from men than Eddie could offer, and this infuriated Cathy, precisely because she shared their sentiments. She wanted someone to dispute the obvious, to show her she was wrong. Instead, when she broke up with Eddie, for example, and called her friend Sarah for sympathy, all she got was this bored, resigned voice coming over the line saying, "Oh, it happens all the time, Cathy, it's like the weather. All men are like that."

But even if that were true, Cathy thought peevishly, it didn't mean she had to accept it. We live in the late twentieth century, after all, she said to herself. We can change things if we don't like them. What about climate control and artificial grass?

Cathy had moved to Boulder two years before, enticed by its burgeoning high-tech job market and the promise of unequaled skiing nearby. With her expertise in a specialized field of the data-processing industry, she quickly had found a position with a large manufacturer of computer products. On weekdays, her schedule seldom varied. Lithe and trim, with pale features and long blond hair, she exercised every morning before breakfast and then drove to the low-slung, anonymous-looking headquarters of the Traikon Corporation, where she worked. Throughout the long Colorado winters she went skiing every weekend, usually alone, driving as far away as Steamboat Springs, Snowmass, or Crested Butte. After two days on the glistening slopes she felt rejuvenated. Driving home on Sunday nights through the mountains she sensed the immensities of rock and forest sail past her outside the dark car window, and she made up songs to sing aloud, drumming with her fingertips on the steering wheel.

The summer months always were less satisfying. Lethargic and drained from working indoors all day long, she nevertheless would hover around the television set at home, drink in hand, until after a week or two she felt restless enough to deal with Boulder's teeming night life, whereupon she soon retreated to her apartment and the cycle would begin anew.

As time went by, she insulated herself by providing for a private realm within, like a bed of leaves at the center of a forest, to which she returned more and more often. By the beginning of her third year in Boulder she was seeing markedly fewer people than before, but instead of making her lonely, this isolation encouraged the development of a vigorous new identity which she equated with self-sufficiency. It appeared like a spore inside her and grew until, far from feeling cheated by solitude, she looked forward to the end of the day. Only when alone was she unconstrained and at ease. She sang to herself, invented make-believe companions, exercised, or read books until it was time for bed.

Sometimes, after a week of seeing no one but her coworkers at Traikon (where she tested various components of a telecommunications processor known as a digital telephone voice multiplexor) Cathy began to feel light-headed, as if she were dissolving in order to release what lay deep inside her. An effervescence filled her body with a light, expectant quiver. She would find herself sitting motionless on the sofa in her living room. The sofa faced a little balcony four stories above ground, and looked out over the tops of large cotton-wood trees to the mountains in the distance. She would stare off into space with the sensation of floating, as if she had the gift of being lighter than air.

Once, after she had been sick for five days with the flu and, staying home from work, had seen no one else at all, a strange thing happened. The curtains over the sliding door were open and, although early evening, it was still light outside. She felt herself brusquely forced through the glass door and out into the air past the balcony where she hovered—arms extended, stomach arched, legs curved backward—like a figurehead on the bow of an old sailing ship. She felt as if she had two bodies: one sat with knees crossed on the sofa while the other hovered in the air outside, certain, sooner or later, to become aware of itself and plunge to the ground. Frightened and disoriented, she found herself saying over and over in a plaintive whisper, "I must be going crazy. . . ."

In an effort to dispel this sensation she stood up and went into the bedroom. Pausing before the mirror over the dresser, she forced herself to breathe slowly and regularly as she enumerated what she saw—the straight hair brushed back behind her ears, the angular face made sallow by fever, the large blue eyes staring intently—until she became one person again.

During the weeks that followed, Cathy was unable to forget this experience. Sitting with someone in a bar, or at work during the day, she replayed it in her thoughts.

And finally she realized that her discomfort at the time—her fear of insanity—masked what actually had been going on. Because now, she had to admit how much it had excited her, how vital she had felt.

Then, one night at home after dinner, as she forced herself to watch television, she felt a restlessness build inside her until she couldn't keep still. It was toward the end of October, not long before the first snow of the year comes to the high country west of Boulder. She had been having trouble sleeping lately, and was counting the days until six months' absence from the ski slopes finally would come to an end. She turned off the television and began pacing around the room. From somewhere in the apartment house came the sound of music, and the wind in the trees through the half-open balcony door ebbed and flowed like the sea. Riding a swell of nervous anticipation, Cathy was moving around in a directionless swirl when she noticed the broom which stood against the doorjamb leading into the kitchen. It was a beautiful, sturdy corn broom with a yellow wooden handle. She ran to get it, then pushed aside the furniture and rolled up the carpet. And then, standing erect in the living room—exasperated and uncertain of what was going on—Cathy began to sweep, and as she swept she could feel herself blushing.

"God, this is so embarrassing," she murmured. But soon, in spite of her thoughts, she was grasping the handle of the broom lightly as she fell into an easy rhythm of long, fluid strokes, rocking forward onto the ball of one foot and back onto her opposite heel. At each return the broom clicked over the same spot on the hardwood floor. As she continued, the strokes became more extensive and uninhibited. They were magnificent gestures, devoid of restraint but at the same time effortless and relaxed. The head of the broom reached upward until, with each pass, it softly brushed the ceiling. On and on she swept, first from the right side and then from the left, her arms and face wet with perspiration and her heart pounding, until she felt lifted off her feet with each returning stroke.

"Cathy is sailing," she exclaimed, giggling and laughing. She repeated the words in a full clear voice until she lost track of herself. The music in the distance had stopped, but outside the wind was blowing hard. She could hear, on the branches of the trees, the masses of leaves as they tumbled over each other. She felt a tremendous rush, a surge of invincibility similar to the moment-to-moment adjustments of balance while hurtling downhill on skis. The following morning she awoke on the floor next to her bed, muscles sore and hair drenched in sweat. The broom lay beside her.

Every night thereafter Cathy swept, aware of nothing but her laboring breath, her vacant mind. These sessions transformed her. During them she lost all but the most fundamental sense of the passage of time, gliding imperceptibly through its momentum like the stars through the sky. She rarely felt fatigued now, no matter how little she slept. In order to move freely while sweeping, she bought a pattern and a few yards of muslin and made a long loose-fitting smock, like a caftan. By the time another month had gone by she had given up going to the singles bars. She stopped dating men and, after taking off two weekends in order to ski, she stopped that too, discouraged by the noise and the crowds. Instead, Cathy stayed at home.

"I guess my friends are going to be upset when they realize I'm not seeing them anymore," she told herself, but she no longer cared about that. She realized that a big change had taken place in her life as a result of sweeping. She had progressed from having friends and not being satisfied with them to not needing them anymore. "If people find out I don't have any friends, they'll think I'm weird," she said, and looking fixedly into the mirror she saw the corners of her mouth form a slight and distant smile.

Other changes were taking place as well. The tedium of her job at Traikon ceased to bother her. Periods of mental exhaustion which had been a problem in the past virtually disappeared, as did the troublesome embarrassment she had felt because of the uncreative nature of her work. On the other hand, relations deteriorated with her fellow employees in the Communications Division. Cathy was bright and capable; for several months she diligently had been attending classes in computer design and business management provided by the company. It was taken for granted that those who could do so would try to move up in rank in the corporate structure, educating themselves for positions of increased responsibility while they continued to work full time. But such priorities no longer interested Cathy. She quit the classes, and when called into personnel to discuss the situation she said she was content doing what she did and just wanted to be left alone.

At the same time, she came to see those around her at Traikon as actors who had taken roles in a sort of extended school play. It was as if they had been assigned their parts on condition they first allowed themselves to be put to sleep so they wouldn't notice that, in the long run, their careers were going to take on the unbroken inevitability of dreams. She fantasized stepping up to an especially fatuous fellow employee she knew and, without warning, clapping her hands in his face, as if to awaken him. Something of this new attitude made itself felt, and the result was a subdued resentment toward her, as if she thought herself too good for the company she kept. The handful of acquaintances she had made over the course of two years at Traikon drifted away, and she did nothing to retrieve them. Cathy was happy. She looked forward to her nightly sessions with the enthusiasm of an astronaut preparing for lift-off. Anything else she was obliged to do became a thankless task.

It was late Sunday evening, three days after Thanksgiving, and because of the holidays, Cathy had been sweeping until dawn for four nights in succession. She was far inside her routine, the broom swishing softly back and forth, her weight transferred timelessly from one foot to the other, a cold breeze ruffling the curtains over the balcony door (for she liked fresh air while she swept, regardless of the temperature), when suddenly there came a loud knock at the door. After a moment of silence it was repeated. At first Cathy thought the sound came from somewhere inside her, and when she stopped sweeping it was with the disoriented sense of having been forcibly awakened from a deep sleep. Without thinking, she went to the door and opened it. In the harsh fluorescent light of the hallway stood a man in a blue terrycloth robe and slippers. He looked to be in his late twenties, about Cathy's own age. He had closely cropped brown hair and was clean-shaven.

"Hi, I'm Dave," he said. "Dave Wheeler. I live downstairs."

"Downstairs?"

Cathy stared at him, dazed and self-conscious. Dressed in her muslin smock, she held the broom upright in one hand while sweat poured down her face and arms. She found herself looking at the monogram on the breast pocket of his robe. "D-B-W" it announced in large florid letters.

Dave Wheeler's eyes widened as they took in the smock and the broom. An unsettling thought he couldn't quite articulate began to form inside his head.

"Yeah, I live on the third floor, in the apartment directly below you." He grimaced, then paused, uncertain how to proceed.

"Look," he said apologetically, "I'm sorry to bother you, but whatever you're doing up here is keeping me awake. It's nearly midnight now, and I have to go to work tomorrow. The floorboards move, or something, because the ceiling in my place creaks in the most maddening way, over and over. It isn't that loud, but it's been going on for weeks now and I can't block it out. I've been meaning to come up here before this, but. . . ." His voice trailed off.

"I'm exercising," Cathy finally blurted out, not

knowing what else to say, and this seemed to reassure him.

"Oh, heck," he said, nodding sympathetically, "you're in training. Why didn't you say so? Well, listen, do you mind trying it in another room? Can't you exercise during the day?"

He said nothing further, because she stood without moving, a hard, unsociable look on her face. At first she had been mortified by the thought that, for more than a month already, someone had been listening while she swept. Even though he obviously couldn't have known what she was doing, it had struck her as an almost physical violation of her privacy. But now that the implications of the situation were clear, she felt completely exasperated. She pictured herself trying to continue the sessions and knew it would be impossible. She would be inhibited from now on by the presence of this jerk below her, no matter what he thought was going on. He had ruined everything.

"I'll work on it," she growled abruptly, and shut the door in his face.

Cathy walked back into the darkened living room and listlessly pulled the curtains open. Moonlight came across the floor, bathing everything in its milky glow. She sat down on the sofa and looked across the room at the blank silent screen of the television on its stand. The perspiration drying on her body made her feel cold for the first time that night; taking a woolen shawl which was draped over the back of the sofa, she put it around her shoulders. She couldn't believe that, with one knock at the door, someone of whose existence she hadn't even been aware was able to upset her life so completely. Sinking into a mood of despair, she sensed her eyes grow moist and had to force herself not to cry. It would be necessary to find another place to live—a small house, perhaps, with no one above or below her, no one to listen while she swept. Single houses were expensive and hard to come by in the tight Boulder market, but Cathy decided she would rent one nonetheless: it was the only way she saw to regain her liberty.

During the coming weeks she read the listings in the newspaper and made appointments with realtors. The prices asked were ridiculously high. Most of the houses she saw were quite small, with narrow, cramped back yards and neighbors' kitchens which seemed to be no more than twenty feet away. There was less privacy in them than in her apartment. But each place she saw only increased her determination to find the right one, for, just as she had suspected, ever since Dave Wheeler's visit she had been unable to do any sweeping. She had found it impossible to fall asleep and had even gone out and gotten drunk a couple of times, with predictable results. She decided to look in the countryside east of Boulder, beyond the suburban housing developments and colonies of condominiums. She didn't care if her neighbors on the dry, lonely plains might be poker-faced ranchers who drove around in pickup trucks outfitted with gun racks, or if she would be without the security provided by apartment managers and lighted streets: she vowed to have a house of her own, someplace with a garden and trees, and a fence around it.

Finally, on the weekend before Christmas, eight

miles outside of Boulder on a dirt road between stubble-covered cornfields, Cathy found what she wanted. It was a small, one-story grey clapboard ex-farmhouse on the property of a farmer named Bob Ordway, who lived with his family in a modern house a half-mile up the road. Ordway, in his sixties, was tall and thin, with sparse sandy hair and a narrow face. He seemed curiously preoccupied, as if a voice only he could hear kept calling to him. While they talked, leaning against Cathy's car in the driveway, he stared intently across the empty fields in a disconcerting manner, monitoring some invisible situation. But when she expressed a serious interest in the house he snapped out of his trance and methodically took her around, demonstrating how everything worked and showing her what needed to be fixed.

"You know, this place is full up with memories," he said in a flat, washed-out voice, a voice almost totally without affect, as if explaining something to himself for the hundredth time. "For the longest while we wasn't gonna rent it out. But nostalgia don't pay the bills, am I right?" He said all this while staring at the knuckles on his right hand.

Nearly hidden from the road by a stand of Russian olive trees and a few old cottonwoods, the house was of an anonymous, modest type fast becoming rare in Boulder County. It had a faded vine trellis on the south wall under the bedroom window, an overgrown yard with a cement birdbath in the center, and a little white porch which sagged into the ground and was in need of paint.

He unlocked the front door and they walked inside. The house hadn't been lived in for some time and smelled quite musty, but it looked clean. Its only real drawback, as far as Cathy could see, were the low ceilings and small rooms: her broom was sure to hit the walls if she really let go while sweeping. But when they stepped outside again into the yard, she looked up at the enormous sky above her and realized she could sweep right there where she stood. Colorado's semi-arid climate guaranteed many clear nights, the crisp air would be marvelous, and in winter she could dress warmly in her down jacket and mittens; once she got going, she wouldn't notice the cold.

Although the prospect of sweeping under the stars thrilled her, it brought with it a twinge of uneasiness. The nearest cluster of condominiums was more than a mile away, its lights hidden from Ordway's property by low hills, but someone passing by on a moonlit night might see, through the line of Russian olives, a lone figure in the dark yard, swinging a broom back and forth with long, fluid strokes. Nevertheless, perhaps more shrubbery could be planted, or a fence put up beside the road. The problem could be solved, Cathy decided—where there's a will there's a way—and she looked forward impatiently to the first of January, when she would be free to move in.

Bob Ordway finally understood Cathy was going to rent the house. He looked directly at her for the first time and smiled.

"This place is perfect," he suddenly remarked with enthusiasm while she was writing out the deposit check. "If you was out driving on a Sunday afternoon and saw it setting here under the trees, you'd surely say to yourself, 'Now *there's* a fine home to raise a family in' . . . . Plenty of room for horses, and the pond out back can be stocked with fish in the spring. By the time the corn comes up you'll have hundreds of songbirds around here, it's like living on a cloud, their music is so beautiful. I'm sure you and Mr. Houghton will just love it here," he declared emphatically, then stopped short.

They eyed each other uncomfortably. Then he winked, encouraging her to laugh along with him as he drawled, "You mean to tell me a nice-looking young lady like yourself ain't married yet?"

"I live alone," Cathy replied gravely, and although she meant it as a simple statement of fact, something grainy in her voice made him break away from the conversation and stare off across the fields again, silent and uneasy, giving all his attention to whatever it was he saw out there.

Out West and Back East

Out West

One at a time, the armed men come down dusty, winding gullies to the steeper arroyos, the spurs on their boots glinting in the afternoon sunlight. They descend gulches to the floor of the canyon, a thin band of trees and rock that winds along the creekside. Sixteen men who have never seen one another before, but who are expecting one another, since no one else would care to make the journey to this canyon, or is even aware of its existence.

On a narrow strip of sand, alongside a little high country creek rushing vigorously to nowhere, the sixteen men assemble in a tight group, take off their hats and shirts, and unhook their belts and holsters, letting their sidearms drop to the ground. All are natives of the rural Western states, successful ranchers and farmers in their fifties and sixties, some of them silver-haired now but still self-possessed and self-reliant. Their hearts are set to pounding by the ritualistic atmosphere which comes to prevail below the rim of this remote plateau in southeastern Utah, among this group of strangers. The late afternoon sun burns into their leathery faces as, one by one, the men kneel softly in the sand and silently begin to pummel one another with their fists, lunging as far as their reach allows while remaining upright.

By turning in all directions some can strike four or five of their neighbors, while others are able to hit only one. Tears of exertion and emotion pour down their faces as, after three hours, half-dead with fatigue and dripping blood and perspiration, the men lower their fists and embrace one another, weeping with harsh guttural cries, like lava and brimstone wrenched from the center of the earth.

Several more hours pass, filled with awkward embrace, during which the sun sets and an intense high country cold comes to replace it. The men are now trembling from dehydration, cold, and hunger, the traces of their passions drying on bare backs until the strong winds pouring down from the plateau bring wild silvery dreams of pneumonia, fever, and death.

They control themselves around midnight, knees swollen, stomachs knotted, mouths filled with dust and gravel. Staggering to their feet, shivering and numb, they locate holsters and belts, strap them to their waists, put on shirts and hats and, with their eyes, wordlessly bid eloquent goodbyes, each one eventually finding and taking the steep path he had arrived on some twelve hours earlier.

Meanwhile, above all this, in a loose circle stretching out for several miles along the canyon's lip, the late-model four-wheel-drive vehicles stand parked in readiness, engines running. Inside them sit the wives of the sixteen armed men, who at this very moment are working their way slowly up the various gullies and arroyos leading away from the canyon floor. The prim, severely marcelled wives sit patiently in heated compartments, steam rising off open coffee containers as they wind plaid blankets closer around their knees, otherwise motionless in the front seats of jeeps and pickups and vans, calmly waiting.

Back East

It is early Sunday morning. Three men, dressed in armed forces-green jumpsuits and scuffed black paratroop boots, form a slowly rotating triangle on the closely packed dance floor of The Galaxy, a private club consisting of one cavernous room with the entire universe projected along its walls and ceiling, located on the twelfth floor of a lower Manhattan loft building.

Ira is a successful copywriter in an advertising agency, Jeff an ingenue actor, and Bruce a veteran Korean chef. They first met a little over a year ago and have been nearly inseparable since. Come Friday at about nine o'clock in the evening, Bruce, Jeff, and Ira usually find themselves together until the following Sunday afternoon, and this weekend has been no exception. The varied permutations of three distinct personalities and physiques have served to entertain and give pleasure for two nights running: during visits to numerous clubs and bars they have caroused, laughed, and made love. At The Galaxy since midnight, they will remain until it closes, sometime before eleven in the morning.

As the song "Dancin' with Myself" booms through the vast hall the three men lose themselves in the push of the music, a sensation as invigorating as fording a swift and powerful river. In spite of the hour they feel freshly alive, the week's routines and irritations having long since been dispersed in deafening sound and the closeness of each other's company. Their thoughts repeatedly float off to the middle of nowhere. Disinterested, becalmed fantasies take place, unrelated to present surroundings and companions. Bruce, 41 years old, dreams of his childhood home, an isolated trading town in the stony, rain-soaked mountains of coastal South Korea; Jeff, 22, sees the mischievous, adolescent faces of his high school friends in Beverly, Iowa; and Ira, 29, gloats over memories of various strangers, Asian, African, and European men, partners in casual affairs he has had during the summer vacations he looks forward to taking each year.

Entwined within itself, arms draped over shoulders, this triad moves along the floor in a long, curving line, describing a path of sorts through countless dancing couples. Around it people mill and smile, argue and embrace. Faces and bodies leave their imprints on the attention of the three men like life forms encountered underwater, calling up a myriad of responses only to disappear, replaced by others. They have not slept since Thursday night but pills, dinners and shows, cocaine and liquor have served to keep them enthusiastic, and by now they feel an immense euphoria, seemingly impervious to the passage of time and their own fatigue.

Seen from the railed-in balcony on the mezzanine above, Bruce, Jeff, and Ira advance along a wide arc through the roiling crowd, as if tracing a small segment of the vast orbit of their lives. Far above their heads planets and constellations are projected, while periodically a velvety white moon rises, temporarily dimming the prickly light of the thousands of stars enfolding them. The path of companionship, their progress seems to be saying, is a long and curious one, along which they will rotate through the walls of The Galaxy, out into the streets, and onto the track of time itself. Dreaming alone while laced for support in the arms of their friends, the three men huddle together, eyes half-closed, distant smiles on their lips, as the couples immediately around them on the dance floor pause to take in this novel configuration, pondering its many possibilities, weighing the chances for its survival.

Lorenzo's Collection

Lorenzo is a quiet, even-tempered man of independent means who has come to accept full-fledged addiction to his playthings. Waking up in the middle of the night, he stares across his moonlit room at the changing assortment of objects and scenes which periodically lights up before him on the floor. Lorenzo doesn't like to leave his bed, and hasn't been outside the confines of his high-rise apartment, on East 28th Street in midtown Manhattan, for more than a year now, although in recent weeks the thought that he may never give up collecting has made him uneasy.

The dozen or so situations which comprise his collection at any one time resemble dioramas: they materialize without warning and sit glowing in the corners of his room. Although he can't make them appear, those he ignores eventually fade away. A few, like surviving inhabitants of an eidetic zoo, run back and forth along the big, blank apartment house windows which look into the sky from the 22nd floor. Some have been with him for months. Others, like the herd of miniature ponies galloping headlong into the wainscoting, vanish moments after he takes notice of them. As he lies in bed on this particular evening, an unseasonably warm and dry one in May, Lorenzo sees:

—A caped and quilted rabbit, over four feet tall, with festive tablecloth eyes, a pink pincushion nose, and aluminum foil ears. It stands holding a volume of Horace securely in its paws, and every so often reads aloud: "Why not beneath a tall plane tree or this pine here recline at ease? . . . They change their sky, but not their mind, who run across the sea . . . ." After an hour has passed the rabbit lays the book aside and makes a tour of Lorenzo's room, dropping ashes from the sleeves of its cape as it goes. Lorenzo is certain, after a night spent observing its movements, that this singular creature wanders around the room perfectly at random, returning to take up its book only when its red and white checked eyes happen to come into direct contact with Lorenzo's.

—A flat-faced, middle-aged man wearing a blue serge suit and sandals who holds a tightly rolled Russian language newspaper, occasionally slapping it impatiently against his open palm. "Sergei!" a frumpily dressed woman beside him calls out in a hoarse, congested voice. Since she doesn't face her companion when saying this, Lorenzo can't determine precisely who is being addressed. She tugs at the black babushka around her head with one hand while balancing, in the other, a large can with the four-color picture of a sunflower on its side. Thick-set figures in shapeless overcoats hurry past the couple on their square of sidewalk, taking no notice of them. The man and woman seem to be waiting for a bus: they crane their necks in the same direction. They are life-size, however, so the red plastic bus circling Lorenzo's room every fifteen minutes, no bigger than a Pekinese dog, is unable to stop and pick them up.

—A black cast-iron elephant which never moves from its circle of bright yellow light. Around its feet, steam rises from a grating in the floor and evaporates in the air, as from city streets after rain. Originally the elephant was an opaque presence in his room, but soon patches of reddish-brown rust formed on its flanks. They glowed in the spotlight like nebulous masses of floating algae. As oxidation from the steam continued, the corrosion began to take on shapes which stood out more and more clearly, and Lorenzo found himself being treated to a visual primer on evolution. Mutating animal life progressed from simple to sophisticated forms. This evening, Lorenzo sees a stocky man naked to the waist who wears a crumpled fedora and brandishes a handgun. With the appearance of this man, Lorenzo's elephant has briefly come alive. The trunk jerks restively, the tail crackles with pent-up energy, he can see sweat on its shoulders and smell its mustiness. The stocky man with dusty, sweat-stained body and powerful hands, perhaps the animal's trainer, raises his revolver and aims it at Lorenzo's calm, attentive face.

—An olive-green, commercial size, twin washer-dryer appliance. The completion of its wash cycle is followed by five minutes of silence, whereupon the half-hour cycle of the dryer begins. The water gurgling through its system reminds Lorenzo of a swiftly flowing mountain stream. The dryer has its own sound, as well:

nests being constructed by a swarm of hyperactive blackbirds. After the appliance shuts down, the door of the dryer flies open revealing a yellow shirtsleeve, while a puddle of dirty water spreads across the floor from underneath the washer. At this point, the overhead fluorescent light fixtures short out, crackling and fizzing. Lorenzo looks on in fascination as irregularly illuminated reflections from the other things in his room ripple across the surface of the water. The smell of the sea reaches him and he shudders involuntarily. He wants to get out of bed and go down to the street—he sees himself striding along 28th Street, startled by the reflection of his face in shop windows—but this restlessness soon passes and he settles back against his pillow with a deep exhalation of breath.

—An elaborately equipped fishtank on a long metal stand, its size and variety of tropical fish suggesting a municipal aquarium. Occasionally visible among the moss-covered rocks are small men and women in wetsuits who are souvenir hunting by aqualung. The brilliantly colored fish elude them. The divers must content themselves with collecting bits of coral and exotic, microscopic seashells. Their purposeful activity contrasts with that of the fish, which look well fed, and never seem to be doing anything more than cruising. Above the gentle waves, a rocky coastline along the rear wall of the tank supports a series of colored postcards of rambling old seaside hotels from the turn of the century, structures with extensive balconies and ornately carved eaves. In between these, one or two unattractive modern resorts can be glimpsed, revealing sections of plate glass, cyclone fence, and whitewashed concrete.

—A small portable refrigerator wedged between cupboards in the cramped galley of an ocean-going yacht. The galley sways violently back and forth, the sound of breaking crockery is heard, and finally the door of the refrigerator slams open. Inside is a mason jar with a label affixed to it which reads, "I Will Remember This Moment Forever!" Faint cries of alarm escape now and then from the jar.

—A dentist's drill, chair, instrument tray, and washstand: the entire operating module in white porcelain, complete with towels, clamps, pliers, a trellis-like affair holding rows of dentures; a young redhaired dental assistant with protruding eyes who appears beside the chair; and the dentist himself. Whenever Lorenzo looks over at the "Dental Corner" of his collection, this dentist—a tall robust man, tanned and fit—strides busily into the room, clucking and chattering as he stores his set of golf clubs by the washstand. He dons a blue nylon smock and starts to prepare little cups of fillings. The assistant beckons to Lorenzo. The dentist smiles gaily and asks after Lorenzo's family. Before receiving a reply he begins a softly interminable monologue about baseball, politics, the weather, air pollution, racing cars, interest rates, parking permits, *nouvelle cuisine*, and fly casting. On those rare occasions of forgetfulness when, dubiously, Lorenzo eases out of bed and seats himself in the chair, the assistant pounces on him with a hypodermic needle while the dentist holds down his shoulders. Wanting to cry out, Lorenzo is struck dumb by the size of the needle. The redhaired girl with bulging sea-green eyes makes no attempt to apply the pain-killer locally, to the teeth and gums, but instead drills the contents of the ampule directly into his brain. When Lorenzo regains consciousness sometime later, the dentist and his assistant are gone. The chair, drill, and other equipment gleam silently. Returning to his bed, Lorenzo leans back on his pillow and stares vacantly across the room, gingerly touching the top of his head, then his jaw and lips.

—Soon, something new catches his eye: ranks of black soldiers who advance, in unending waves, through an African savannah to the distant horizon. They are dressed in tropical uniforms: knee socks, shorts, and starched bush jackets. The only note of color is the red braid visible here and there on shoulders and helmets. The infantrymen's forward progress never slackens or varies, and the sun, although low in the western sky, does not succeed in going down. This continuously extended moment of humanity on the march, breathtaking in its uncompromising severity, instills in Lorenzo a sense of foreboding. Their fury will know no bounds, he thinks, when the members of this army finally realize no orders exist for them to come to a halt. Thorn trees, snakes, insects, and wild animals take their toll on the men, so that although battle with an adversary never occurs, the ragged touches of red seen among the smallest and most distant of them—among those in the front lines—forcefully remind Lorenzo of the wounds of war.

—A gymnasium built of cast iron and glass, whose massive facade gives an impression of grand scale, like a structure housing botanical gardens or a nineteenth-century Crystal Palace. Visible within its thousands of hexagonal windows are courts for basketball, handball, and tennis, as well as an eight-lane swimming pool, steam rooms, saunas, and a hardwood running track. Gymnastic equipment stands about: rowing machines, punching bags, trampolines, and barbells. The building is animated by a constantly shifting population of dark mustachioed men, many of them in poor physical condition. In spite of this, however, they run and jump, tug, pull, and punch in a dedicated manner. Weaving among them are the establishment's attendants, dressed in billowing orange pantaloons. These attendants provide the men with whatever they might need: fresh towels, adhesive tape, snacks, and even cigarettes, which many throughout the hall puff on while they exert themselves. The gymnasium is as busy as an old-time railway station. From what Lorenzo can make out, the men inside it are Bulgarians or Romanians or Turks. Stony-faced with athletic purpose, they persist for hours at a stretch in a slow and stately manner. Once in a while a gymnast pauses to rest, peering out one of the windows in the direction of Lorenzo's bed. At such times Lorenzo sees a swarthy, phlegmatic-looking man of advanced age, with a long silken mustache and large, sad, purple-rimmed, tobacco-colored eyes. On occasion, when one of the men stops and looks outside, Lorenzo waves, and even throws bits of balled-up paper, but so far he has had no response. The silent figure soon turns away and rejoins his companions.

—Micki Wainwright, American housewife. She sits

alone at a breakfast nook in the corner of her suburban kitchen, dressed in a white satin morning coat and slippers, stirring a cup of coffee. She is waiting for someone to join her. Steam rises from her cup, as well as from the full pot of hot coffee on a warming plate in the center of the table. The other cup, resting on its saucer on a yellow plastic placemat, is empty. Macramé wall hangings and potted plants surround the picture window which looks out on her back lawn from above the sink and its spotless drainboard. A red phone hangs on the wall next to her. Periodically it rings and she picks up the receiver: "Micki Wainwright speaking," she announces in a self-consciously cheerful voice. Then after a moment, with a stiff smile, she extends the receiver toward Lorenzo as if inviting him to bear witness, and he hears a dial tone which continues for a short time until a loud, oscillating whine interrupts it. He makes no move in response. Soon Micki's smile disappears, replaced by an unreadable expression. She returns the receiver to its cradle on the wall. Her hands shaking from caffeine, or from some less apparent source, she pours herself another cup and settles back in her seat to wait.

—A busy office, down a long hallway off a suite of other offices, on the 36th floor of the Raymer Building north of Madison Square in Manhattan. Within this room, whose doorway looks over desk tops and through a window at vistas of distant metal towers, four women are working for a large commercial firm. Heavy-set, hair streaked with grey, cashmere sweaters draped over their shoulders and wearing eyeglasses attached to gold chains, the women look matronly and self-assured. They have worked in the same office for nearly a decade, but their images of one another are at variance with the images they have of themselves, so that, although they function well professionally, they dislike and distrust one another. Imagined or real slights, plots and intrigue constitute, in the stream of daily events, a permanent undertow which would go unnoticed by any casual visitor to this cramped, effervescent cubicle. Lorenzo, however, has been an onlooker here for longer than anywhere else in his collection. He has come to know these four women intimately, at least during office hours. Two are black, two white. Often they dress in contrasting outfits, the black women wearing white and the white, black. In the complicated games of office politics played among them, sides are frequently, but not always, chosen according to skin color. At such times Lorenzo glimpses, through the open doorway, pairs of matching faces huddled together in conspiracy. A principal cause of friction concerns possession of the favorite desk, situated nearest the window. While the others are preoccupied, one will lay claim to this desk, only to have her belongings removed from it when she steps out of the room, or her chair pulled from under her as she stands talking on the telephone. Pranks, schemes, and sabotage are always in the air, ranging from pilfered apples to attempts at canceling another's salary line. The lengths to which the women go in order to camouflage their intentions, the artfulness with which mischief is concealed in the business at hand, long ago made Lorenzo an ardent fan of this little office, and made of it a place he anticipates returning to with enthusiasm, as if to the first day of work at a new job.

—Five blocks of Madison Avenue, from 34th Street to 39th Street. Lorenzo sees, as he looks up one side of the avenue and down the other, storefronts, office buildings, and a few brownstone houses. He pauses before the grimy Gothic Revival Church of the Incarnation Episcopal, on the east side of the avenue between 35th and 36th Streets, then keeps pace with a group of perspiring high school students in shirtsleeves who carry satchels of books and wool blazers as they walk slowly uphill toward the Morgan Library. In the past he often visited this sprawling white marble palazzo with its collection of rare prints and manuscripts. As he reaches the corner he is tempted to turn off the avenue and walk down 36th Street to the entrance. Today, however, he would obtain little satisfaction from viewing such assemblages: they would only remind him of the mute hoardings of childhood. Instead, he resumes walking north on Madison until he reaches a handsome Victorian brownstone, now the headquarters of the Lutheran Church in America, on the southeast corner of 37th Street. This was once the residence of J. P. Morgan, Jr., who communicated with the collection he administered at the Library by way of a garden between the two properties. Lorenzo stares intently at this house for some time, memorizing the color of its blocks of stone and graceful first floor windows with their wrought-iron balustrades, allowing himself to see, barely visible between heavy curtains, the face of the long-vanished financier. He then turns away and looks back down

Madison Avenue. Clusters of people walk along, leaving doorways, crossing sidewalks, getting into taxis and buses. Lorenzo feels the warmth of the sun on his face. He hears voices of nearby pedestrians and watches the traffic signals changing from red to green, one by one, as automobiles and trucks come toward him up the avenue. It's four o'clock or so on a weekday afternoon in May. Soon the traffic lanes will become congested, and an avalanche of workers from the surrounding buildings will descend onto the avenue, pouring along pavements and over curbs, buoyant and expansive, joking with one another, full of expectation for the approaching night.

Lorenzo ambles slowly back down Madison. By the time he crosses 34th Street he has become aware of feeling lighter than air, of being detached from the crowds of shoppers and increasingly heavy traffic. At the corner of 28th Street he turns left and approaches the red canopy over the sidewalk in front of his apartment house. Even though it's been a warm day, now in the late afternoon shadow of the big buildings a cool wind is blowing, and Lorenzo shivers involuntarily. He would be very surprised to learn that the two people standing under the canopy at the curb as he passes by are convinced he is being self-consciously hip when he turns up his white shirt collar against the wind, and the little pointed wings jut forward along the sides of his face. He doesn't notice them smirking at each other as he quickens his pace and strides into the entranceway.

Once inside, he crosses the nondescript lobby and presses the brass knob beside the elevator doors. A bell rings and the metal doors slide open. Nodding hello to a small, silver-haired old woman with a distracted look under her lilac-colored beret who steps uncertainly out of the elevator, Lorenzo gets inside and pushes the button for the 22nd floor. Letting himself into his apartment with the single key on a rabbit's-foot key ring, he moves from one room to the next, switching on lights. Finally he opens the bedroom door and walks in. He sees himself lying propped up in bed, his arms resting on a yellow wool blanket tucked neatly under the mattress. He is staring fixedly at a bare spot on the hardwood floor, but at the sound of the door being opened he looks up abruptly and peers across the room at the newest member of his collection—the silent figure of Lorenzo, a troubled look on his face, his shirt collar turned up and his hands thrust deep in his pants pockets, standing by the open door.

Music from the Evening of the World

In the large old apartment filled with heavy furniture, high above Park Avenue, Mrs. Simpson tended her assortment of hot water bottles scattered, like red rubber hearts, on the sofas, mahogany tables, and voluminous easy chairs which took up corners and vantage points of every room. Nearsighted and short of breath, she moved on swollen legs in a practiced yet difficult routine which took her through shuttered rooms and along dimly lit hallways whose velvet-covered walls ended in baroque gilt cornices and ceilings grimy from years of inattention. Her schedule, established some time ago, demanded that shortly after breakfast she fill a series of kettles with water from the tap and bring them to a boil, one by one, on her beautiful old gas range dating from the Gay Nineties which squatted like a monument behind the marble prep table running along the center of the kitchen. Each kettle, if not left boiling for too long, contained enough hot water to fill five of the rubber bottles. In addition to carrying a kettle with which to fill them, she also had to take along a receptacle for the tepid water already inside them. Since there were dozens of bottles throughout the apartment, Mrs.

Simpson had found it most manageable to complete her task in an unvarying manner. She always began in the library, which overlooked the avenue, at the front of the apartment. Her daily allotment of physical vitality, meager enough when compared with the amount of work which lay ahead of her, seemed to last most satisfactorily if she started with the rooms furthest from the kitchen, saving the pantries and hallways closest in for the end, when her legs felt like lead weights and the ringing in her ears began to alarm her. Exhausted, discouraged by the prospect of time gaining on her even as she had finished, for the moment, all there was to do, she would sink onto one of the stools in the kitchen, drink a glass of bouillon brewed from water portioned out of the final two or three kettles, and contemplate the rest of her day. She calculated her remaining strength with the intuition of a veteran chemist and, depending on what she thought possible, after a short nap would go to the hairdresser's or the movies, or, if the weather was fair, to the zoo.

The worst times, however, worse even than running out of energy halfway through the round of bottles waiting to be filled, were those late afternoon hours when Mrs. Simpson returned alone from her forays into the city. Entering the ornately decorated lobby of her apartment building always seemed to intimidate her, even though the doorman's inquiries after her health could have sounded in her ears from a voice deep in a dream, so well did she know it; and the maintenance men, the elevator boy, and building manager, all belonged to a cast of characters who had played their parts in an identical fashion for years. Even variations in this routine came off without hitches or unexpected dialogue. She could have sleepwalked through Christmas, for example, because each year, on the fifteenth of December, the decorated tree always went up in the lobby, between the smoked mirrors to the left and the long benches of black leather and chrome. Easter Sunday occurred when the doorman changed his dark winter uniform for a tan one with white piping, and the Fourth of July always found the men, for the first time, in shirtsleeves, suddenly full of sarcastic remarks about the bare legs of young women who passed along the sidewalk outside the entrance. Nevertheless, the late afternoon returns to the apartment were difficult for her. Greeting the doorman, entering the lobby, taking the elevator to the eleventh floor, bidding the boy good day as he stopped the car and pulled back the sliding door, her mind never wavered from a single image, which grew more intense as she neared her apartment and fit the key into the lock. She pictured the cold rubber bottles as they would look when she opened the door: lumpy objects lying inert on the furniture, several of them glowing in the quiet emptiness of early evening in the apartment, at the onset of another night alone.

Sometimes, though, when she grew tired of her customary procedure, so tired she couldn't bear it anymore, Mrs. Simpson steeled her nerves as if for a long march across alien territory and left the apartment instead of retiring to bed, no matter how late the hour, no matter how her ravaged body would rebel the following morning. Getting into a taxi the night man flagged off the avenue for her, she would order the driver to take her to the infamous Club de Lys. She had found a matchbook from this club among her husband's effects, and out of curiosity had decided one night to go there. Since then, she had returned several times. Such excursions, though infrequent, constituted almost her only form of indulgence. Though she no longer smoked, she brought cigarettes to hold unlighted, because everyone smoked in the Club de Lys. Though she no longer danced, she wore a long formal dress under her fur coat, and gave attention to making up her face, and took out the strands of pearls Mr. Simpson had given her years before, because everyone dressed for the Club de Lys. She was able to lose herself there and become engrossed in its ambience and clientele, certain she would never in a thousand years meet any friends from her previous long life with her husband in such a place.

An elegant motif at the door and in the foyer of cinnamon-colored flamingos on a silvery floral background abruptly gave way, after the cloakroom, to a rectangular space furnished with dilapidated pink Naugahyde banquettes along its walls. Two rows of small round wrought-iron cafe tables were placed down the center, each surrounded by uncomfortable-looking chairs, rickety and covered in black vinyl, with heart-shaped wire backs. Next to the bar, in the corner nearest the entrance, was a fishtank filled with tropical fish; above it, several large red-and-white striped umbrellas were pinned awkwardly to the wall. A dirty beveled mirror hung behind the bar, and at several places in the room candy-cane columns spiraled to the ceiling for structural support. At the far end stood the stage. Well-heeled, formally dressed patrons wandered about, making their way back and forth from the bar to their seats in a wary, guarded daze, as if thrown together on the deck of a ship after the accidental release inside it of some dangerous chemical.

Mrs. Simpson always sat at a table by herself. Ordering a cocktail from the waiter, she settled back against her wire heart and peered around the room, thankful she wasn't noticed in return: the couples in attendance—portly middle-aged men, for the most part, accompanied by younger women—were entirely taken up with each other. Although her eyes gave her trouble, so that she frequently had to rest them, Mrs. Simpson liked to observe these couples, watching their expressions as they chatted, smoked, drank, and occasionally cast involuntary glances toward the darkened stage at the front of the room. Their faces intrigued her: they were like puzzles. The longer she looked at them, the more she began to see problems and contradictions. She tried to guess, in each instance, the nature of the relationship prevailing between two people sitting together. Were the women married to the men they accompanied, or merely companions? Were elements of trust and sharing present, or was the relationship evanescent, metallic, strained? Very rarely did she feel certain enough of her impressions to come to a definite conclusion.

After several visits to the Club de Lys she realized that it wasn't simply a question of being unable to tell how these people related to each other—they also seemed alien to her, as if composed of some strange new material, something dense and opaque. This was why she had so much trouble interpreting the signals given off by them—people were so different now than in the past. And there were so many more of them now than thirty or forty years ago. The world was far more crowded, everyone jammed together, which caused people, as a defensive reaction, to camouflage their behavior, and created that great need for distraction she saw in the faces at the Club de Lys, and elsewhere too, for that matter. Because the places she knew outside New York had changed just as drastically over the years—the coastline of the Greek island where Mr. Simpson and she went on their honeymoon had been hardly recognizable when they returned in 1980, what with all the condominiums, the motorboats and tourists. Even the little fishing village in Maine where they spent their summers—what a shock it had been to see it suddenly submerged, one Fourth of July weekend, in bumper-to-bumper traffic. Why, back when they had bought their cabin by the sea, the road that wound alongside it had barely existed. Now that same road conveyed a never-ending stream of automobiles crawling along the "scenic route." It really appeared, sometimes, as if the world had burst at the seams, and all the people who inhabited it had become oddly fugitive strangers.

As she sipped her drink in the Club de Lys and sat with the unlighted cigarette in her hand, Mrs. Simpson thought back on the last time she had seen her husband. Tall and rotund, seemingly in good spirits, betraying no sign until just before he left the apartment of any variation in his daily routine, he had dressed for the office, read the morning paper with breakfast, and joked with her about the hot water bottles. But as he paused at the door while she completed the ritual of helping him on with his overcoat and handing him his briefcase, he had stared, suddenly and directly, into her eyes, with an unswerving glance so unlike him that she became alarmed. He then kissed her passionately on the lips, thrusting his tongue deep inside her mouth, a thing he had not done for at least twenty years, if he had ever done it before. He left without saying goodbye. And when, distraught, she had walked back to the dining room, the letter announcing that he was leaving her, and explaining precisely what he wanted of her, lay on the plate at his place, neatly typed, next to a single remaining wedge of buttered toast, slightly burned the way he liked it. Mrs. Simpson was at a loss to explain his behavior. Like all unions of long duration, theirs had witnessed certain strains through the years, but she had fully expected, without ever really considering it, that they would remain together until the end. Now, she didn't know what to think. She telephoned his office several times during the day but he didn't put in an appearance there, and toward evening she lay down the receiver, giving up hope of seeing him again. The firm where he had worked for 27 years seemed disinclined to pursue his disappearance, other than to report it, as a matter of record, to the police, because the day Mr. Simpson failed to show up had been the last day of work before his retirement.

In the letter he declared he was leaving her. He gave no reason, but stated that her life should go on as before. His lawyers were empowered to take care of her needs, but remained in ignorance of his whereabouts. She needn't try to find him, such an effort would only prove fruitless. He had been planning this move for years, he wrote, and with his customary deliberateness had thought it completely through. He had taken care of every detail, anticipated every possible development. She was free to do whatever she liked, so long as the apartment continued to be maintained in the manner to which they both had grown accustomed. She would be looked after financially provided that she never divorced him, and never left New York City except for two months in the summer, from the weekend following the Fourth of July to the weekend after Labor Day, when she was to have use of their cabin outside Bar Harbor. In addition, she was obliged to set a table for two, every morning, and prepare his favorite breakfast, even though he no longer would be there to eat it. She was at liberty to take dinner by herself. Finally, she must continue to meet the daily challenge of keeping the water bottles hot. No maids or other help were to be hired for this purpose. She must do it herself. On this point he was quite adamant.

This chore of hers had originated in a moment of giddiness one New Year's morning a decade before, and as time went by Arthur Simpson had approved of it more and more strongly. In his letter to her, he reminded her of his membership on the advisory boards of numerous philanthropic institutions, above all those concerned with the preservation of the world's environment. "You see, my dear," he wrote in closing, "knowing that you are faithfully executing your marvellous ritual with the water bottles will comfort and reassure me. It will forcefully bring to mind, wherever I may be, the plight of so many of our fellow creatures on this earth, like the wonderful sea turtles we saw on the coast of Quintana Roo in Mexico, remember them? As they continue to lay their eggs in vain on the crowded tourist beaches, their inability to change in the face of new conditions—their dignified, ungainly, doomed attempt to perpetuate the old ways—serves as a lesson to us all, a chastening reminder of the folly of staying put."

After Arthur Simpson had vanished, this ritual became the center of Mrs. Simpson's existence, the anchor to which the ship of her days was tied. Inquiries to her husband's lawyers revealed everything to be as he had written: they indeed had charge of a sum of money with which her needs were to be met. All the rest he had taken with him. She was free to go to court in order to contest his instructions. In fact, his lawyers were of the opinion that if she did so, she certainly would gain control of the entire sum left to her. Nevertheless, that amount really was not very large, and as they were bound to defend his interests vigorously, she would be obliged, in turn, to engage lawyers of her own. When she won, what remained might no longer suffice to support her. In that sense, they told her, such an action on her part would not have the result she perhaps anticipated.

A final round of drinks was served to the patrons at the Club de Lys as the house grew dark and spotlights bathed the stage. A nubile young woman, whose beautiful body was naked except for an old man's long white beard and a wig of tangled flowing grey hair, strode toward the plain wooden table and chair which were the only props. In one hand she held a brass bugle. Rising on tiptoe, she brought it to her lips and gave a short blast. She then stepped back and unrolled a blue satin scroll on which the words "Modern Love" were embossed, bowed briefly to the audience, and ran between the tables toward the back of the room, disappearing behind the bar. After a few moments two lithe, muscular men of similar height and build walked onstage. They too were naked. Over their heads they wore elaborate wigs above expertly detailed and colored shoulder-length latex hoods. One sat down on the chair while the other stood leaning against the table. Several minutes later, when the room had settled and become quiet, the one who was sitting stood up and began to run his fingers through the other's hair. His face, that of Marilyn Monroe, was fixed in a dazzling smile, as if she were posing for a publicity photo. The thin red straps of an evening gown, her creamy white shoulders and beautiful satiny blond hair, contributed to a most unnerving presence when coupled with the actor's pale, sweaty, unadorned male body, which diminished and looked neutral in comparison. The man whose hair she caressed wore John F. Kennedy's face, smiling self-consciously as if basking in the glow of sustained applause. It was the crisp, self-assured, slightly manic smile of the career politician, extroverted and manly. His hood included the lapels and shoulders of a blue business suit, a fresh white shirt, and patterned tie.

As Marilyn lovingly and attentively stroked JFK's hair, he became increasingly agitated, finally pushing her arms aside and turning on his heel away from her. She gave out a squeal of alarm and circled around him, sinking to her knees and locking her elbows around his legs. But JFK broke free and strutted around the stage, miming various negative responses to her wordless en-treaties, and at one point making as if to leave the stage entirely. Marilyn went down on her knees again, her hands linked together in supplication, but JFK was impervious to this gesture. Ignoring her, he stood facing the audience and preened himself, while that broad smile sailed out in alarming isolation across the room. Abruptly, however, the chemistry between them changed: Marilyn stood up, impatient and tense, her silken hair swinging in the light, and thrust out her chest, daring him to respond. Now it was she who pre-tended to walk out, while JFK, his body shivering and pale, beads of sweat rolling down his back and the se-vere part in his wig becoming unglued, mutely pleaded with her to stay. He followed her across the stage, trying to impress her and once more gain the upper hand, but she only teased him in return, repeatedly slipping out of his grasp at the last second. The act, which had begun and continued without a word being uttered, ended as the figures embraced feverishly over the table, JFK fall-ing backwards onto it while Marilyn, by now physically aroused, her stiffened penis swinging against his hip, climbed on top of him and covered his chest and head with kisses, her long blond hair finally obscuring his face until, with a crash, the table gave way under their weight and, to accompanying cries of abandon, the stage went black.

Mrs. Simpson hardly bothered to watch this exhibition, which had remained the same each time she had seen it. Indeed, the only variations were unplanned: occasionally a member of the audience, possessed by patriotic outrage, disrupted the proceedings, lunging drunkenly onstage. Employees of the club waited in the wings specifically to put an end to such interruptions. But the rest of the audience never failed to react in a predictable manner. Their sighs and surprised exclamations began with the bearded herald and continued after the two actors were gone and the houselights had come up, at which time they shifted in their seats and stole embarrassed glances at one another. Gradually, however, their discomfort was supplanted by the appearance of a final member of the cast. Attention turned toward the stage where a diminutive page-boy appeared, carrying a tray filled with cigarettes and dressed in the instantly recognizable cap and uniform of the figure from the old Philip Morris advertisements. He began moving slowly through the room. As he approached each table, the people sitting at it stopped talking to stare at him. Mrs. Simpson smiled to herself, remembering the mixed emotions she herself had felt the first time he had come close to her, swinging his tray back and forth and calling out in a low-voiced parody of the original. For in spite of his small size and slim, compact body, his dry sagging cheeks and the lines around his eyes betrayed his age. The boy standing before them was at least fifty years old.

The page-boy's approach to her table invariably suggested to Mrs. Simpson that it was time to go home. His blue eyes, pale as southern skies in winter, reminded her of Mr. Simpson's, and she thought once again about her husband. She still couldn't picture him in this place, yet she had known when she found the matchbook that he must have come. Perhaps it was this discrepancy which brought her back here, although she always told herself, when still at home, that she would go to the Club de Lys to watch the people's faces while they, in turn, looked at the show. She had long since grown tired of the same presentation, and wished she possessed the energy to attend the second performance, which began at two a.m., and which, Mrs. Simpson knew, was different in content from the first one. But she never had stayed to see it. Her schedule and her age wouldn't permit her to do so. Besides, the longer she sat in this smoke-filled room the more her eyes bothered her.

Leaving a large tip for the waiter and excusing herself from the patrons surrounding her with a shy smile, she slowly rose to her feet and made for the exit, coat–check in hand. Once in the taxi which took her home, she found herself racing up a nearly deserted Park Avenue just ahead of the lights. They turned from green to yellow one by one as she watched them from the back seat, her eyes growing pleasantly heavy with sleep, her body feeling composed and snug inside the long fur coat which fell, in warm luxurious folds, to the black rubber mat on the floor.

Ronald Colman

Ronald Colman was not the screen star who graced such films as *If I Were King* and *A Double Life*. "Hollywood" was the disparaging name he gave his fifth-floor walkup apartment on East 6th Street off Avenue A in Manhattan. He had adopted the name Ronald Colman as the result of a fateful encounter with Mr. Ronald Colman of Brooklyn, New York. The son of Irish immigrants, Mr. Colman was a wholesale chemicals-and-dyes salesman who never married, never caused trouble or stood out from his fellow citizens, except inadvertently, and passed away in 1973. One day in November, 1963, shortly before his retirement from the chemicals-and-dyes company, Mr. Colman crossed 14th Street at Seventh Avenue, in Manhattan. The man who was walking ahead of him, cradling a transistor radio at his ear, stopped in his tracks and began shouting incoherently and weeping. Mr. Colman, fearful at first that the man had taken leave of his senses, soon joined the other pedestrians in the vicinity, crying and beating his temples with his fists, as vehicular traffic came to a halt and everyone mourned the newly fallen President, John F. Kennedy.

Beside him at the curb on the southeast corner of 14th Street stood a twenty-two-year-old woman named Rosa Antinori and her four-year-old son Carlo. Newly arrived in America from the Abruzzi countryside and unable to speak a word of English, they were terrified by the violent gestures that suddenly erupted around them. People dropped shopping bags and other belongings and pitched about as if on the deck of a storm-tossed ship at sea. Carlo was trampled by a trio of wild-looking black women with panic-stricken eyes. Rosa attempted to make sense of what was happening, tugging at elbows and asking, "*Che cosa?*"

Carlo implored her to explain what was taking place. Without thinking, she spoke aloud the words "Ronald Colman" in a thick Italian accent, as if they might coax meaning out of the uproar. She had noticed these words stamped in gold block letters on the bulky sample case that the salesman, in his grief, had dropped beside her on the sidewalk. Soon they were swept away by the animated crowd, but not before Carlo fastened on these syllables and repeated them as he and his mother made their way into the darkness of the subway station to return to their tenement apartment on Division Street. Again he asked her what was happening to them. Her lack of response finally made his face turn white. His body went rigid and he repeated "Ronald Colman" over and over in a stubborn monotone as they held each other tightly on the packed subway car.

Rosa had come to America to escape the memory of her husband, Guiseppe, who had died in a farm accident outside the town of Sulmona. Survival had been difficult enough up to this point, since the only people she could turn to were the Mastrocettis, her husband's distant cousins, who lived in Paterson, New Jersey. Her work as a seamstress in a nonunion shop necessitated long hours away from home, and Rosa found she no longer could cope with a child. In the ensuing months their situation deteriorated to the point where, one snowy morning in February, 1964, Rosa agreed with her husband's cousins' plan to surrender the child for adoption. (Later she would marry a man named John Loviglio and move to Chicago, where she gave birth to other children and forced herself to forget.)

Carlo moved in with the Meyer Frankenfeld family in the Bronx, joining six Jewish brothers, younger as well as older than he, whose names and faces he sometimes could not keep straight. After an initial period of estrangement he felt accepted by this busy, prosperous, yet curiously detached family. He attended school and helped at Mr. Frankenfeld's string of dry-cleaning plants. The onset of puberty seemed to disturb Carlo, however. He ceased to communicate except for outbursts of surly negativity, which repulsed his surrogate parents to the extent that they did nothing to pursue him when one day at the start of the tenth grade he packed a suitcase with some clothes and ran away. Moving to Manhattan, he survived as a dishwasher, delivery boy, and handyman, never lasting more than a few months at any job because of his antisocial behavior.

The mid-1970s found Carlo living on East 6th Street under the name Ronald Colman, selling vegetables out of a small storefront on 7th Street that he rented from a man named Lon Kotman, who was descended from Silesian peasants. As Lon understood it, the Kotmans had migrated in 1889 from the town of Ostrava, then part of the Austro-Hungarian Empire, to southwestern Pennsylvania, where they bought farmland. After his discharge from the army in 1957, Lon left Uniontown for New York City. He operated a restaurant until he saved enough money to buy two buildings on 7th Street with several business associates.

Lon's grandfather, Karl Kotman, though purportedly Silesian, actually was from Bukovina, in the Ukraine, and a Jew, who hid this fact for five years from his wife, the former Mina Leventhal, a raven-haired girl he met in Brno in 1883. Mina, headstrong and intractable, in revolt against her impossibly strict shopkeeper parents, Teufel and Elena Leventhal, acted the rebel during her adolescence and married Karl principally to infuriate her parents, since at the time everyone believed that he was not Jewish. Actually, Karl Kotman had been born Lev Koppelman. After they had moved to the United States, Karl and Mina used to laugh about those days, although they did not return to the religion of their youth, and raised their children as Roman Catholics.

But Karl never revealed to her the reason he had changed his name and concealed his background: not from the fear of religious persecution common at the time but rather from embarrassment. He was mortified by the memory of the poverty he had endured as a child in Bukovina and the shame of being raised in a broken home. His father, Moise, had abandoned his young wife and their three children in the tiny hamlet of Chaldo-

wywe, near Poland, in 1868, running away with an itin-
erant theatrical troupe "direct from Paris, France,"
composed for the most part of alcoholic former music-
hall singers from Prague. After unsavory adventures involving local theatrical producers and constabulary
throughout Central Europe, Moise arrived in Paris in
March, 1871, with two of the original members of the
troupe, just in time to find himself hurled into the dangerous days and nights of the Paris Commune.

Quickly adding to the little French he had acquired
while with the troupe, Moise survived the Commune
by abandoning his life as a fledgling actor and melting
into the ancient Jewish community on the Rue des Rosi-
ers, in the Marais. With the onset of the Third Republic
and the return of relative normalcy to civic life, Moise
settled down on the Rue du Temple, opening a tailor
shop under the name Moise Remberg. After marriage to
Hermione Solas, a young Parisian Jewess from an established family, he returned to carpentry—the love of his
early youth—and organized an atelier specializing in
the manufacture and repair of fine furniture.

The business prospered. Soon Moise Remberg was a
successful member of the Parisian haute bourgeoisie,
known and respected outside the close-knit, isolated
Jewish community. Parlaying funds from his commercial enterprises into real estate by means of contacts he
had made with local politicians, before the end of the
century he became one of the wealthiest men in Paris.
His only disappointment in life was the inability of Hermione to bear more than one son; young Leon Remberg
was not suited for management of the extensive, rather

complicated Remberg business ventures.

Though quite intelligent, from an early age Leon had shown not the slightest interest in the aggressive behavior of normal boyhood, preferring instead to inhabit the world of his imagination. He grew up with his collections of stamps and toys, venturing out of the house only to school and to the numerous museums of Paris. Above all he loved the National Conservatory of Arts and Crafts, on the Rue Saint-Martin, so near where he lived that he stopped there almost daily on his way home from school. He was fascinated by the exhibits and would stand for hours in front of Foucault's pendulum, which demonstrated the rotation of the earth, or in the room full of wonderful automata, such as Marie Antoinette's clockwork dulcimer-playing puppet, which he was secretly convinced he resembled.

Leon was a withdrawn boy but also a stubborn one, and as he matured, he took perverse pleasure in doing whatever he knew would frustrate or disappoint his father. By the time he was twenty, he had passed with surprising ease through a range of dissolute activities about which his father, never having exposed himself to them, could only generalize in a negative fashion.

The first years of this century saw Leon living alone, ignored and finally disowned by his family after his scandalous attempt to blackmail one of Louis Lumière's nephews. He had become obsessed with the fledgling technology of motion pictures and had hoped somehow to seize control of the Lumière machine by threatening to expose the sexual irregularities of this nephew. Instead, Leon found himself, for the first time, alone and without means of support. He survived for several years among the nocturnal idiosyncrasies of life along the boulevards below Place Pigalle. In the early morning of July 11, 1912, he was found dead in the courtyard of his hotel, a crumbling structure off the Boulevard Saint-Denis, after having persuaded a young English traveler to accompany him to his room.

The Englishman, John Farrell, of Sheffield, the son of a hardworking cutler of modest means, had recently fled to France to escape a gambling debt. He was living from day to day in a state of foreboding brought on not so much by the money he owed as by the panicky feeling that he did not know himself. His adventure at the gambling table in Brighton had upset him; always believing that his luck was about to change, he had continued to place bets long after he should have quit. He would never forget the look of pity in the eyes of the other men at the table as that evening had drawn to a close. It had perplexed and infuriated him.

Without a penny to his name, and speaking almost no French, he was gratified by the offer of temporary shelter from a sympathetic older man. When Leon Remberg could not contain himself and revealed the true nature of his interest, Farrell was overcome with rage and, without realizing what he was doing, stabbed him in the chest. As Leon fell to the courtyard pavement, Farrell came to his senses. His only hope lay in flight. Luck seemed to be with him, and before the morning was out, he had robbed a young woman at knifepoint and boarded the train to Calais. He returned to England and settled in London's East End, where he was working as an apprentice lorry mechanic under the name Roger Corbett when the First World War erupted in Europe. Although no one had seen the murder take place and it was never solved, Farrell did not know this, and he could not forget what had happened. In his determination to avoid being sent to France as a soldier, he obtained forged identity papers using a second alias, Frederick Upton, and migrated to Canada just before Great Britain entered the war, leaving behind him a girl named Mary Chester, who was pregnant with their child.

Mary Chester grew up on a farm in the North Country, and her parents were so poor and morally unyielding as to rule out her return home in her condition. Deserted without warning by the man she was expecting to marry, Mary nevertheless proved resilient. In Covent Garden one day, she met an elderly Scottish woman living on a fixed income. First establishing the common bond of the soil—she and the distinguished lady had lived not fifty miles from each other, Mary growing up northwest of Newcastle, while the family seat of her new-found friend lay below Galashiels, in the Southern Uplands—Mary found herself chatting with someone whose unpretentious manner and gentle sense of humor seemed miraculous. She insinuated herself into the woman's heart with her tale of love and abandonment, and before an hour was out had found a new home. Mrs. Mac Ewan, as the elderly woman was called, claimed she needed a housemaid and decided then and there that Mary would do perfectly. Several months later a cherubic girl was born. The child, christened Norma Corbett, took up residence with her mother in Mrs. Mac Ewan's modest house in South Kensington, and grew up thinking that her father had perished at Verdun.

A delicately beautiful child with golden hair, at ten years of age Norma began to have a recurrent dream of riding in a white coach across the heavens. This coach was driven by a handsome man whose back was always turned; the two splendid horses he guided seemed to hurtle themselves sideways along the sky, almost as if they were traveling upside down but at incalculable speeds. Norma emerged from these dreams feeling dazed and unable to concentrate on school. Most of her schoolmates were jealous of her beauty, and by the age of sixteen she had only one friend, a girl of comparable attractiveness, Marjorie Ruggles. Marjorie was determined, despite fierce opposition from her family, to be an actress, and it was through her that Norma became involved in the theatre, whose pitfalls and peculiar commitments she never fully understood. Her passion for the stage outdistanced her modest abilities, and she was to suffer numerous disappointments on the road to her goal.

London in the thirties was a difficult place for her. Soon after Mrs. Mac Ewan's death, Norma's mother married a widower from Birmingham with three children and was gone as well, though letters containing small banknotes continued to arrive sporadically, along with packages of crumbled Cornish pastry. Norma was working as a salesgirl in a large, gloomy department store on Tottenham Court Road when, at the Soho rehearsal hall where she and her friends read aloud from George Bernard Shaw, she met a young American actor who changed her life, Richard Rideout.

Lustful but otherwise sullen and quite unsympathetic, Rideout soon was back in the United States with Norma in tow. Although she did not love him, Norma had been prepared to put up with a good deal in order to escape her life in London. But Rideout insisted that she remain in their shabby hotel room on West 39th Street, in Manhattan, while he disappeared for days at a time, supposedly in search of work. After two weeks had gone by in this fashion, she left the room every morning to discover, in spite of her disorientation and intimidation by the city, some connection with a new life.

Haunting the theatrical district, she made the acquaintance of several struggling young actors, two of whom, Bill Pierce and Beverly Ann Simmons, disclosed to her their plan to sell their possessions and move to California to begin new careers in the cinema. Norma decided to join them. To pay for her bus ticket, she pawned the little jewelry she had brought with her. When Rideout turned up at the hotel room the evening she was to leave, he seemed to feel guilty about the precariousness of her situation and relieved to have her off his hands. Unexpectedly, he gave her twenty dollars for the journey west, which Norma interpreted as a sign of good things to come. She and Richard parted informally and never saw each other again.

Overjoyed, she ran down into the street with her suitcase, looking forward to her first large meal in days during the several hours that remained before she was to meet her friends at the bus station. She had walked no more than a block, however, when she came upon a movie palace whose lights glowed like those of an ocean liner. The marquee announced the New York premiere of *The Prisoner of Zenda*, starring Ronald Colman, Madeleine Carroll, and Douglas Fairbanks, Jr. Realizing she had enough time to see it, Norma contented herself with a hot sausage from a nearby sidewalk cart, bought a ticket, and went inside.

She was enthralled by Colman's performance as Rudolph Rassendyll, the noble, self-sacrificing English hero who assumes the guise of his double, the abducted crown prince Rudolph of Ruritania, in order to prevent a takeover of the throne. While impersonating the kidnapped prince at his coronation, Rassendyll falls in love with his future queen, Flavia, played by Madeleine Carroll. Before the movie ended, Norma thought that, with her own clear features and golden hair, she resembled Miss Carroll closely enough to note the producer's name, David O. Selznick, and determine to make his acquaintance as soon as she arrived in Hollywood.

Ronald Colman had been born in 1891 in Richmond, Surrey, England. He took part in amateur dramatics while working for the British Steamship Company. Invalided out of the First World War, he went onto the stage professionally. He was successful and made a few films in Britain before coming to America, in 1920. While working in the New York theatre, he was seen by Henry King and chosen to play opposite Lillian Gish in *The White Sister*. Samuel Goldwyn put him under contract, and Colman quickly became a star.

As an actor he was not troubled by the advent of sound. When he spoke, he revealed himself as charming and urbane. His mustache and his manners cast him perfectly as the mature, forthright romantic, and as such he won a large following. He discovered how consistent underplaying could work for him, and he took care to preserve his looks. After *Kismet* (1944), he worked less and less, and retired in 1949, returning only for two cameo roles—in *Around the World in 80 Days* and *The Story of Mankind*. He passed away in 1958.

The Town by the River

Although we had little to say to each other, I always
looked forward to seeing Lara Mitchell. Her bulky features and impassive manner, the oversized flannel shirts
and shapeless, faded trousers she wore, never failed to
evoke in me a strong feeling I associated with the 1940s.
Lara and I had been young then. She still lived in Winfield, the town in Massachusetts where we grew up,
while I had spent many years away from it. But since
returning to Winfield, it was Lara Mitchell's presence
which mattered most to me, because she alone seemed
to activate images of those days in my mind's eye.

I'd begun seeing these images two years before,
while living on the West Coast. At first they simply involved memories of people with whom I'd been ac-
quainted as a child in the forties, but gradually those
gave way to reveries of people and places I didn't know
at all. As long as I thought of them as arbitrary—as spon-
taneous after-effects of magazines and newsreels seen
years ago, echoes of landscapes traveled through, or
streets glimpsed momentarily—I could feel comfortable with these reveries which, after all, took place rather
infrequently, separated by days and weeks of ordinary

life. However, shortly before leaving the West Coast, I discovered they weren't the result of chance associations but instead were intimately related to one another. I saw something with exceptional clarity one day, and it made me realize, as I paid close attention to its details and atmosphere, that all this time I'd been seeing images from one particular place and time in the past.

A group of men and boys, whom I took to be fathers and sons, descended a hill toward a grass ball field on what seemed like a leisurely Sunday afternoon in late spring. Gloves, bats, and balls in hand, they came down from the neighborhoods in the town above. It was a sleepy town, resting like a soft, tree-lined checkerboard on a rise overlooking a placid river. The river was wide and slow-moving, its muddy banks beginning just past the outfield of the diamond at the edge of a municipal park.

I came to know elements in the life of this town quite well. Although I couldn't identify with it, since I'd never lived in or even visited it, the town definitely existed. I'd seen enough of its inhabitants to be certain of that. It was a small town on a river somewhere in the Central States, possibly in Missouri or Illinois or Indiana, a town whose side streets I often had walked, past houses in whose backyards I had stood, in whose ponds and creeks I had fished.

Its appearances before my eyes were triggered, without warning, during the most ordinary moments. Putting down a newspaper or finishing a drink, looking up as a woman walked by or a group of men stood arguing on a street corner, I suddenly would find myself once again in that place, sometime during the 1940s—an un-noticed bystander, an onlooker barely present while ev-eryday situations unfolded around me. A hairdo, a look in someone's eye, the turn of an ankle beneath a plain cloth coat, certain buildings, groups of pedestrians or conversations overheard—these things led me to a van-ished era, to experiences I was sure weren't actually mine, in the sense that I'd ever lived them during the years in question. I became intrigued, even obsessed by them, but trying to force the town to appear was invari-ably unsuccessful. Instead, I had to be in an absent-minded and receptive mood, thinking of nothing in particular, oblivious to the passage of time and of what was going on around me, before they revealed themselves.

My great discovery upon returning to Winfield was that, in some inexplicable way, Lara Mitchell served as a catalyst or lightning rod for my experiences in the town by the river. Although she remained a taciturn New Englander, reserved and suspicious to a fault, because we'd known and liked each other long ago she now felt at ease with me. She didn't seem to mind sitting quietly over a coffee or a beer while I stared past her into the middle distance, free from the burden of having to carry on a conversation. The reveries which arose at these moments usually were comprised of small groups of people at work or rest. Sequences unfolded, ordinary and perhaps uninteresting in themselves, which were apt to vanish from sight at the next mo-ment: an ancient pickup truck, its windows opaque with frost, which came toward me down a deserted street on an early winter evening; a sunny, open, un-adorned town square, the air parched with dust from a summer windstorm, at the edge of which two farmers, in from the country for the day, made room for me on a wooden park bench; an elderly couple in their garden, dressed in sweat-stained workshirts and floppy straw hats, who leaned on their hoes, squinting into the sun-light . . . .

And, rarely, the same extended episode involving a woman in her late twenties, a stranger to me. She entered a curtained upstairs bedroom in a house on a quiet residential street, took off her plain cloth coat and rumpled, plaid flannel dress with its old-fashioned lace collar, unpinned her hair, and lay down on the thin cotton chenille bedspread beside me.

By the time I returned to Massachusetts to live I wanted nothing more than to understand these experiences. By recollecting in detail all the times I had seen her I tried to identify the woman who lay down beside me, and this led me back to our very first encounter.

I was living in a suburb of San Diego then, teaching American literature at a branch of the University of California. In addition, in my spare time, I was preparing the text for a cassette tape, as well as for a handbook to be published in braille. The text detailed job opportunities for the blind in high-technology industries where, because of their lack of specialized training, they did not think to look for work. Several months before this, Mark Gillette, a friend from the university who was a designer of computer programs, became convinced that, especially in certain computer-related fields, lack of sight should prove to be an asset rather than a liability. He believed that absence of distraction from the outside world gave a correspondingly greater freedom to visualize complicated programming systems.

Sightless persons often possessed a highly developed ability to picture the world they couldn't see. This allowed them to comprehend, revise, and creatively restructure systems whose subtleties escaped normally sighted people. Working with the blind in a local community outreach program, Mark had discovered their capacity to abstract from limited amounts of data, to operate within a purely conceptual framework. Furthermore, he found that some were capable of handling the heavy volume of reading material necessary to master this new skill in a variety of ways. They were able to take notes in braille with a slate and stylus, or they used the Kurzwell Reading Machine, which scans print and reads it back into tape in a synthesized voice.

I had enough faith in my friend's idea to help him raise several thousand dollars. This enabled us to hire a researcher, whose task it was to scour the trade-related publications and job lists of industries in America which made extensive use of sophisticated computers. Naturally, the list was a long one, especially when government and the far-flung multinationals were included.

The results of this compilation were encouraging, and Mark and I formed a business partnership. He contacted corporations to apprise them of the talent of which they were unaware, while I finished writing the text. We hoped to organize an employment agency and have the book and tape out within a year.

One evening in June, some weeks after spring semester had ended, I drove to a restaurant I liked which overlooked the Coast Highway and the Pacific Ocean, sat down on the terrace, and ordered a drink. It was early for dinner. The first groups of people were just arriving, walking up a curved staircase from the parking lot below to the restaurant's entrance. The sun setting over the ocean cast a coppery, hieratic glow on the faces of the approaching diners.

Suddenly a group of three, obviously a family, came into view along the path from the parking lot. As they mounted the stairs, the father in his oddly formal white dinner jacket and the plump, florid-faced mother vanished from my awareness. All I saw was the daughter, a pale, unwell-looking girl in her early teens, in a long brown silk dress, who walked dutifully behind them. She had dark hair and a dull, pasty complexion, which the sun seemed to get lost in rather than illuminate.

Looking down at this girl, I was transported once again, without warning and in the most unlikely of places, to the forties river town of my reverie. This time, however, instead of finding myself on a street corner or at the edge of a field, I was strolling down a residential street still muggy and wet from a recent rain. I paused for a moment under an enormous maple tree which nearly blocked my way; indeed, sections of sidewalk had been broken by the emergence of roots underneath them. I turned off the sidewalk up a fieldstone path and approached a modest, well-kept two-story grey clapboard house. On the wide wood-floored porch, painted dark green, a white two-seater swing was suspended by chains from the ceiling. Opening the front door, I walked across a faded maroon carpet to the stairs, which I climbed to the second floor. I followed the carpet to a bedroom door, opened it, went in, and closed the door after me. It was dark inside, curtains covered the windows, but once my eyes adjusted, enough light remained for me to see a large four-poster bed at the other end of the room. I took off my jacket and tie and unbuttoned my shirt. Lying down on the white chenille bedspread, I breathed deeply, emptying my mind as I stared up at the dim ochre ceiling.

It was perfectly quiet. Soon the door opened and closed, and a woman I'd never seen before came toward me. Sitting at the edge of the bed, she unpinned her long dark hair, shaking it until it fell down her back, then took off a rumpled plaid flannel dress and lay down beside me. Instead of drawing close to her immediately, I reached across the night table beside the bed and pulled at the curtain until light poured into the room. Turning to look at her I saw she was blind, and while she waited, face tilted expectantly, her body raised on one elbow, I broke into a smile and tears came to my eyes. I felt dizzy, momentarily bicephalous. There I sat on the terrace of a restaurant at the edge of the Pacific Ocean, concerned about the welfare of a woman I was meeting during the 1940s in a town I couldn't even place.

The reveries prior to this one had been more like

daydreams, evasive and temporary, whereas what was occurring now had the richness of genuine reminiscence—except it wasn't *my* reminiscence. The familiarity I sensed but couldn't recognize struck me suddenly, like amnesia. When I became aware again of where I was, looking at the stairs which led to the entrance of the restaurant, the dejected teen-age girl and her parents were gone, and the sun was setting beyond the horizon line, far out over the ocean.

Winfield, Massachusetts, is a town of some twenty thousand people in the south-central part of the state. In spite of growing up there I never thought of it as home, since I'd been abandoned as an infant and brought to Winfield from the state orphanage at Worcester when I was five years old, to be raised by foster parents. I always felt that Harold Ritchie and his wife, Davey, had taken me on primarily as company for their approaching old age. After the youngest of their three children left for college they cast around for something to fill the void and decided on adoption. I was raised with fairness and even a certain reserved affection, but the Ritchies never confused me with their natural offspring, and especially in my teens, family gatherings were painful occasions for me. Now that Harold and Davey were dead and I'd been living elsewhere for many years, Winfield only called up memories of unforgiving winters, a stagnant post–mill town economy, and sparse variations on what I'd come to think of as the typically unyielding New Englander personality.

I remember clearly my elation when I left to go to

college, and I never thought I'd return. But when the partnership with Mark prospered to an unexpected degree, I was able to contemplate moving away from California and my untenured, adjunct teaching position. Our business had evolved into a consulting and counseling firm; Mark and I now spent much of our time traveling to the headquarters of various companies to present our ideas. We also were becoming involved with the federal bureaucracy in Washington in a quest for research funds. Consequently, it mattered little where I lived so long as it was on the East Coast, where most of our operations took place. To my surprise, I found myself thinking of Winfield.

Certain this impulse was merely a reaction to pulling up stakes so often in my life, I arrived one overcast autumn afternoon, convinced a brief stroll down Main Street would cure me forever of the idea of living there. And the town still seemed to have little to recommend it. The few friends I made while growing up had left long before. Cramped vistas of ancient, rundown corner taverns and pool halls, shuttered houses and locked factory gates, the abiding sensation of nothing happening while the town waited for the onset of winter, were enough to make me return to the bus station. But on the way there I ran into Lara Mitchell, and everything changed. As we stood on the sidewalk chatting, I noticed she was having a singular effect on me. I began trembling and sweating, and looking off down Main Street I felt the forties river town close in on me, I saw its dusty streets and buildings instead of Winfield's: battered Oldsmobiles and Studebakers parked at a slant, that dry midwestern heat, the slow shuffle of farmers in faded overalls as they stepped around Lara and me without noticing us, as if we were an obstruction momentarily blocking their path, like a telephone pole or delivery cart. This shimmering vision somehow had been summoned with exceptional clarity out of thin air by Lara's presence, and I decided right then to stay in Winfield in order to be near her. Nothing else mattered to me, although I knew spending time with her wouldn't be easy. I remembered Lara as a person who was touchy and withdrawn to the point of being antisocial.

After a few minutes the town by the river receded from view. We got to talking about Winfield and the past, and I could see she enjoyed it. I told her I was thinking of living in Winfield for a while and asked if she would meet with me every few days, just to hang out, and she said fine.

I found an apartment above the butcher shop on the main square, overlooking the public library and Mariangela's Bakery. Lara and I got together in the afternoons, usually at Frank's, one of the older taverns in the center of town, where she never prevented me from buying the drinks. At other times we climbed into her black and white '68 Impala, its fenders and suspension shot, and scraped along the little country roads outside of town. She drove very slowly, as if making a tour of inspection around private property, while I looked out the window and daydreamed.

Twenty-some years before, we had been neighbors. Lara occasionally had taken care of me when the Ritchies left town on vacation. Once, in the summer of

1954, when I was eleven years old and she was seventeen or eighteen, she had arrived at the house in a state of nervous agitation. While fixing my dinner she refused to tell me what was wrong, but afterwards, in the living room, she produced a pint of whiskey and began drinking steadily until she was drunk. She rambled through loud denunciations of her parents, her teachers, and various acquaintances, accusing them, one after the other, of hypocrisy, cowardice, and sexual perversion. The fury with which she attacked them frightened me. I'd never seen anyone drink the way she did that night.

I found it curious now, given her distaste for its inhabitants, that she had chosen to remain in Winfield all these years. But when she was younger Lara had traveled, characteristically finding people everywhere much the same, and in Winfield at least, she said, she knew how to survive. Seemingly asexual, large, slow, and plain, she lived alone in a patched-up dwelling outside of town, a relic without hot water or indoor plumbing. She made a living as cleaning lady for several taverns. Some years back she'd been a janitor at the local high school, but although she wasn't a threat to the students, she'd been fired after agitation by a group of parents on the pretext that a man was required for the job. Actually, many townspeople distrusted Lara as much as she disliked them. They believed a woman in her forties, unkempt and solitary, who swept out taverns and kept to a night schedule, set a bad example for their children. This sentiment hardly jibed with the well-known fact that a number of these offspring already were accomplished thieves, regularly breaking into schools and offices in the area and trucking their spoils as far away as Worcester, Providence, and Boston.

I soon discovered that Lara's hostility toward Winfield had long ago produced a situation in which she was in the town but not of it. She seemed to have remained principally because of her tremendous indifference to life. While she never would become sufficiently animated to alter the conditions under which she survived, at the same time she had no need to defend or rationalize them. She existed from day to day, apparently without the need for intimate companionship, and was content to keep me company, as she called it, only because I made no demands on her, and because occasionally, when she was in the mood, she liked to tell me stories.

The business Mark and I had started on a shoestring was flourishing and growing increasingly complex. Expansion meant spending more and more hours on the road. The job training program in computer technologies was fast becoming an international phenomenon, while Mark's connections in the academic world assured continued support for research into the visualization process among the blind. Their rich affinity for abstract thought had impressed executives in several computer-related industries, and after an initial period of skepticism they encouraged our efforts.

As the temperature dropped and the snow flew, I wanted nothing else than to be seated in the back of Frank's, staring along the length of the bar into the big frosted windows at the front, a bottle of beer in my hand, while Lara, smoking Chesterfields and drinking bourbon-and-seven, sat impassively across from me. But instead—dressed in a three-piece suit, carrying cases full of slide presentations, cassettes, and samples of braille—I found myself staying for days at a time in anonymous hotel rooms in midtown Manhattan. I tried to master the intricacies of what was, for me, a whole new world of commerce, contracts, and profits, while I dealt with impersonal marketing vice presidents who took advantage of my innocence.

But then the situation changed drastically: recognizing that we might jeopardize our enterprise by lack of business savvy, Mark and I decided to take on another partner. We sold controlling interest in the firm to a man who also became our chief executive officer, giving up certain future considerations for a substantial amount of immediate cash. Mark stayed on as head of research and development while I was left in an advisory position, making suggestions on company policy and style from afar. And now, for the time being at least, I was a man of independent means. Although I welcomed the opportunity to remain in Winfield as long as I liked, this sudden change of fortune also made me apprehensive. I wondered what I would do when the windfall was gone.

Making use of my newfound leisure, I began to frequent the public library across the square from my apartment. I read all I could find on topics I thought might be related to the town by the river, exploring the nature of time, memory, and out-of-body experience. I discovered "eidetic imagery," self-generated mental images having all the qualities of percepts registered by the senses, and therefore seeming to originate in the outside world. I read articles about hypnosis, astral projection, and meditative states. I learned that, in our three-dimensional world, we're unable to perceive time in its totality—according to theoretical physics, time reversal is a distinct possibility. Logically, in fact, there can be no paradox if one simply observes the past and doesn't interact with it. But when someone actually travels to the past or the future, interacts with it, and returns, enormous difficulties arise.

I pursued tachyons and telepathy, Brownian movement and determinism, reincarnation and speaking in tongues. I got lost in the unresolvable quandaries of quantum physics, where investigations into electric charge, parity, and duration at the subatomic level have yielded any number of conflicting theories explaining the relationship between time and matter.

I read all this and more, but after weeks and weeks I was no closer to understanding the town by the river than before I'd gotten my library card. All I knew was that someone entered a darkened bedroom in which I found myself waiting, and lay down beside me. The woman with whom I kept having identical trysts certainly existed, yet I no more knew where she was than who she was. My sense that these experiences took place in the Midwest eventually led me to the world atlas, where I pored over maps of the Central Mississippi Valley states, speculating that the town must lie somewhere along the 40th parallel, on the upper Mississippi

River—Ashburn, La Grange, or Clarksville, Missouri; Rockport or Warsaw, Illinois. But although I knew the place existed, I also was convinced I'd never set eyes on it in the light of day. After all, my glimpses of it were situated in the 1940s. Wherever it was, the town must have grown and changed enough in forty years to be unrecognizable to someone who has seen it only as a fleeting backdrop behind disconnected sequences of unknown townspeople going about their daily lives.

As the months passed, my sessions with Lara Mitchell grew more and more desultory. My heightened receptivity when in her presence remained exhilarating, but new episodes occurred less frequently, and lately Lara had been showing up for our appointments in an irregular fashion. She was beginning to find them a chore. But in spite of this, I couldn't bring myself to reveal my real reason for getting together with her. I knew she'd react negatively. I knew that the day I confessed what actually was going on in my mind would be the last day I sat with her, silently coaxing a personal universe out of the echoes created by the clothes she wore, the way she drank and ate, her gestures and demeanor.

Then, one sunny afternoon at the end of February as we cruised the frozen side streets of town in her Impala, she became unusually loquacious when I asked about acquaintances of our youth. She told me a curious story. It seems that Dr. Robert Avery, a pediatrician for more than thirty years in Winfield, had left behind a series of diaries when he had died, a widower, several years before my return. These diaries, running to many painstakingly handwritten volumes, contained extended, minutely drawn observations of townspeople he had treated when they were children. Lara herself, apparently, had been one of these "subjects," as she called them. Most entries were devoted to exhaustive recollections of every encounter that had taken place over the years between a subject and the doctor himself. Relationships with the town's residents, even if superficial, had lasted for decades, and in his efforts to distinguish among innumerable memories closely resembling one another, Dr. Avery had resorted to a singular method.

Patients he had seen in the forties and fifties surfaced again fifteen or twenty years later. Children who had served as the subjects of rather harmless erotic fantasies on his part reappeared as adult citizens who were scrutinized—perceptively but often quite severely—regarding their physical condition, marital and financial status, political persuasion, and general worth. The moralizing, judgmental nature of the doctor's later comments clashed with his earlier ones and also lessened their interest somewhat, since his lack of generosity narrowed the scope of the stories he had to tell. Nonetheless, according to Lara, when all the entries involving one person were tracked down, a wealth of detail emerged. Dr. Avery's determination to capture the past evidently had known no bounds except those of his memory. If he failed to reach those limits, the entries ended in peevish complaints about advancing age and his declining mental powers.

Whenever his method worked, however, the results supposedly were breathtaking. Coming across someone who intrigued him, with the aid of medical records and previous diary entries, he would construct a mosaic from his encounters with the subject. Then these entries would proliferate, transcending their original focus to become jumping-off points for lengthy reflections on time gone by. Passages of description recreating the subject as a child would give way to the doctor's personal memories, to anecdotes of love and loss, and laments for his own vanished youth. Such meanderings had nothing to do with the person in question, the details of whose life had served, in the end, as a mere catalyst. These excursions into nostalgia would continue until, abruptly, they broke off and the next entry would begin. In fact, it seemed he lost interest in his subjects if he couldn't use them as springboards for private recollections, and therefore restlessly jumped from one to the next.

Lara concluded her story to me that day by explaining how she had managed to get her hands on the diaries. Two weeks before his death, out of the blue, Avery had telephoned to invite her to his home, saying he had a favor to ask. Lara hadn't been his patient since childhood. Habitually suspicious, she agreed to meet him solely to satisfy her curiosity, because, try as she might, Lara couldn't come up with an explanation of why he had made such a phone call to her. She never before had been inside his home, although it was located not five blocks from where she lived. With her gruff manner, her alcoholic's pallor and perpetually stained, shapeless coveralls, she must have dismayed the tartly correct physician, yet he led her to a chair in his front parlor and began talking.

His health was deteriorating rapidly, he confided. Pale and thin, avoiding her eyes while he spoke, coughing and seeming quite uncomfortable, he revealed to her the existence of his diaries. Now that his time had come, he said, he didn't know what to do with them. He didn't even understand why he'd written them. Nevertheless, he felt strongly that someone else should see what he had labored on in isolation for so long. It simply wasn't right to let this rich mine of information fade into obscurity with his death. He was quite adamant about this: he refused to allow the diaries to disappear without a trace, as if they—and he—had never existed at all. And that was why he'd summoned Lara Mitchell. Someone had to know. Someone had to see.

His wife had died many years previously, and no immediate family was left. All his old friends had died off as well. After much reflection he had come to a startling conclusion. Among the townspeople of Winfield—and he had to give the diaries to someone from town, there'd be no point in it otherwise—among everyone who was left, whom he knew personally, Lara Mitchell was the only one he even remotely considered he could trust! Her disdain for everyone in Winfield—her isolation from them—was such that she seemed the person most likely to honor his last request: to read the diaries and then destroy them without showing them to anyone else. Because Dr. Avery hadn't been interested in publication of his material or in any sort of notoriety. He wanted one thing and one thing only, that after he was gone someone would walk the streets of the town with a knowing smile, privy to the secret foibles and failings, the darkest secrets of those people she would meet face to face, day after day—the pillars of the community who, it so happened, treated her with such condescension. Wasn't it grand, he had said to her excitedly, his face blanching, wasn't it elegant! Dr. Avery told Lara that the night he had thought of her he had laughed so hard his heart had almost given out there and then, palpitating and racing out of control, perversely almost denying him the satisfaction of handing over the diaries to her.

Years later, the irony of having been selected by him on the basis of her unsociability still made her chuckle. It was a vindication of her attitude toward her fellow townspeople. She was gratified, as well, that he had detected her strength of character, that he had felt he could trust her. Not for a second, she said, had she ever thought of betraying that trust. Glowingly she informed me that, after reading most of the diaries, and in accordance with his wish, she had destroyed them, burning them in the wood stove at her cabin.

She leaned back against the seat of the Impala with a self-satisfied smile, but, on the contrary, as soon as the words were out of her mouth I just knew she was lying. So little of consequence ever took place in Winfield— so few things had happened in her life—that I simply couldn't conceive of her getting rid of such a treasure of intimate revelation. Instead, I pictured her poring over the diaries, relishing the secrets contained in them. I knew they were still in her possession, and I was determined to read them. I wanted to see the diaries so badly because in them might be found some mention of me.

The following evening, shortly after nine o'clock, I surprised Lara at her cabin on Oleander Road. This consisted of a series of ramshackle rooms which she closed off one by one as winter deepened until she lived, ate, and slept in the kitchen. During the five months we had been seeing each other I hadn't been invited to her home. Indeed, whenever I asked her to visit me in my apartment, she found an excuse not to come. She must have guessed that I persisted in arranging our meetings at Frank's for some reason other than the pleasure of her company, yet she never inquired about it. Her privacy was the most important thing in her life, and so I knew that this invasion of her territory wouldn't be welcome. Even if I were correct in assuming she hadn't destroyed Avery's writings, my demand to see them would be taken as an insult, maybe even bringing our relationship to an end. But the possibility of learning something about my childhood outweighed all other considerations. With the exception of the afternoon I had first run into Lara on my way back to the bus station, nothing else matched the intensity I felt now, as I stood on her porch in the freezing darkness, hammering away at her front door.

She answered cradling a deer rifle in her arms. After she recognized me and let me inside we joked about the weapon, which I knew she never actually had fired. It was extraordinarily hot in the room. The sight of her belongings scattered around—dishes from a recent meal, a flask of whiskey on the table at which she had been eating, magazines and clothes strewn across her bed—made me acutely uncomfortable. I apologized for my presence, explaining that I'd been too impatient to telephone her first. I didn't mention visions to her, or reveries, or the town by the river, I didn't mention the blind woman. Instead I reminded her I was an orphan, ignorant of the circumstances of my birth. I tried to make her see how traumatic this fact was for me. I knew full well, I said, that she'd claimed to have burned the diaries, but the chance I might finally discover something concrete about my past overwhelmed any hesitation I'd had about doubting her word. I begged her to let me see them, promising to reveal their existence to no one.

She stood up as soon as I started talking and began pacing around the little room, her ears turning red. When she moved past me I smelled whiskey on her breath, as well as the unmistakable sweet-and-sour aroma of hibernation. She grinned nervously from ear to ear and I became frightened for a moment, not knowing how she was going to respond. Then she pushed open the door to the next room and emerged, smiling sheepishly, pulling a foot locker along the floor. She opened it with a key from the ring on her belt and lifted the lid. Inside I saw stacks of leather-bound ledger books, their spines covered in green calico. We gave each other one brief, conspiratorial glance and then, laughing delightedly, fell to our knees in front of the open locker and began rummaging through it, Lara's self-consciously loud guffaws echoing around us. Now that the ice was broken and circumstances had forced her to show the diaries to someone else, she was exuberant. Finally sharing her secret made her as giddy as a child.

We spent the hours until dawn together, wading through volume after volume in the unexpected glow of Lara's willingness to share, drinking whiskey and reading aloud long passages from the lives of countless people. I've never been seized with such exaltation as on that night, drunk on the stories of strangers, fascinated by the wayward, perpetually unsatisfied quality of the doctor's attention. Eventually, realizing I was tired and had a headache from the dim, smoky light, I restricted my reading to diaries dating from the early 1950s when, as a boy, I'd been Dr. Avery's patient. I searched in vain for some mention of me.

Throughout the night I'd anticipated finding my name there among so many others. My keen disappointment when it wasn't took me by surprise, and my mood changed rapidly. All I wanted to do now, as I drained the whiskey in my glass, was to leave Lara's cabin as soon as possible. Feeling exhausted and depressed, I mumbled an excuse and stood up to go.

Lara helped me on with my coat. She looked vexed, and saved for the last possible moment the piece of information which—I realized in retrospect—must have been her only reason for ever mentioning the diaries to me in the first place. As I was walking through the door she remarked in a sarcastic, artificially offhand tone of voice that she supposed, since I was so intent on leaving, I had no interest in seeing the part about the orphan boy. She laughed heavily at my excitement as I pushed past her back into the cabin. Lifting the lid to the locker, she soon found the volume for 1944 and opened it to a page in the middle marked with a strip of paper. She sat down on the sofa beside me and I began reading aloud. I soon became so agitated I could hardly keep my voice from breaking.

"May 11, 1944: An unprecedented development, in recent weeks, has taxed to the utmost my meager supply of compassion. It began on the 29th of last month, in the late afternoon, when I received in my office a haggard and ill-at-ease young woman, poorly dressed, who, to top it all off, was completely blind. Of course, the heart opens without hesitation to such unfortunate creatures, and I confess to being quite moved as I watched her fumble across the unfamiliar office to find a seat. I was so struck by this woman's appearance in my office that a minute passed before I became aware of the infant with her: she cradled it, wrapped inside a blanket, in one arm. In the other she held her white cane. I detest feeling uneasy, and so attempted to make her comfortable, asking if she wanted a drink of water. But she sat silently, turning her head this way and that in an uncanny duplication of someone looking around a room. Then the blanket stirred, and immediately her attention moved to what lay inside.

"She pulled a corner free and I saw the little face, red and covered with a rash, no doubt the result of poor hygiene. Perhaps an inadequate diet also was involved. I've seen this condition so often in my years of practice that I almost expect it, even with babies from the most respectable homes. Time and again such infants are brought into my office. Nothing is wrong with them, really; all that's needed is a lecture to the mother on principles of cleanliness and nutrition. Although I don't mind collecting a fee for imparting such information, nevertheless it hardly amounts to challenging work.

"In this instance, however, I was mistaken. With her first apologetic words the poor woman revealed she knew why her baby was suffering. Given her present situation, she said, it couldn't be helped. Nearly destitute, she had no permanent address, and had been traveling from town to town by Greyhound bus in search of someone or other, I never quite got clear exactly who. Now, still not having found him, she had reached the limits of her endurance.

"I must admit I winced as she related all this to me. My outrage at the man who had deserted her was tempered by an acute discomfort at being taken into her confidence. I am not, I almost said aloud, a social worker or policeman. However, soon she revealed the reason for her visit. In spite of the torment it caused her, she was unable to care for her child any longer and, being a stranger in town, had come to me, a pediatrician, for help. Where—how—by what procedure—should she give the baby up for adoption? Did I know of someone with whom she might leave the child?

"Naturally, I do not have the names of qualified persons desiring to adopt a child on the tip of my tongue. After a moment's reflection, I suggested the safest thing to do would be to take it to the state orphanage in Worcester, where formal proceedings might be initiated. One simply couldn't give the child to the first person who showed an interest in it, could one? In the meantime, I said, perhaps she should apply to the county, here in Winfield, for some sort of assistance, although since she wasn't a resident I had no idea if she would qualify.

"She wasn't at all satisfied with my advice, however. She hadn't the time or money to go to Worcester, she said. Even if she had, she felt disinclined to leave her baby in the hands of the authorities there. I suspect she was afraid of the law becoming involved; in any case, there was nothing further I could do. We sat in silence, until I realized she hadn't the money to pay for the consultation. Taking her by the arm and insisting she owed me nothing for my trouble, I guided her out of my office. Thanking me profusely—she really was a very decent woman, anyone could see that—she squeezed my hand in parting and started off down the sidewalk.

"That was the last I saw of her, although, unfortunately, it isn't the conclusion of my story. The following morning, I had just emerged from the operating room after one of the most difficult all-night births I have ever witnessed, when I received a telephone call from my wife. Shortly after eight o'clock, she had found an infant abandoned on the doorstep leading to my office, wrapped in a plaid blanket and howling at the top of its lungs. Although the news left me speechless, I of course knew whose child this was, and if it hadn't been for dear Beryl's frantic demand for assistance I would have notified the authorities immediately. Perhaps the blind woman was still at the bus station. In any case, it shouldn't have been very difficult to find her. But in the ensuing confusion another hour passed before I remembered to contact the police, and by then she was gone. In the two weeks since that time they have tried to track her down, so far without success. It infuriates me, given her handicap, that none of the drivers on duty that morning remember her. I even have been to the station to question them myself, but to no avail. She has vanished without a trace.

"While the local police fumbled through their investigation I didn't remain idle. My wife and I took the infant—a boy, as it turned out—to Worcester, where he has been left in the hands of the state. Although I wish the poor child Godspeed, I trust never to lay eyes on him again, and hope that somehow, somewhere, his mother is made to pay for what must be viewed as the most reprehensible behavior. However, I cannot deny being left, at the same time, with a feeling of pity, and I wonder why some provision hasn't been made in our society to care for such persons. We normal, functioning citizens owe it to ourselves, finally, to come to the aid of those who are helpless—otherwise, how can we call ourselves civilized? At any rate, with one decisive stroke I've managed to do what's right for the little tyke while at the same time washing my hands of the whole sticky affair. I daresay, as far as he is concerned, things will work out for the best . . . ."

Dazed by alcohol and fatigue, I found myself in the yard outside Lara's cabin, stamping my feet and clapping mittened hands in the frigid air, as glints of gunmetal blue slowly came to the sky above Winfield. In spite of what I'd been reading aloud a short time before, when the whiskey was finished Lara had almost immediately slumped over and fallen asleep on the sofa. I was thankful for that, because now I wouldn't have to answer her questions. The diaries explained everything, yet they explained nothing. I still had no idea where, and with whom, I had been in the upstairs bedroom of that grey clapboard house long ago. If the blind woman was my mother, then who was I? My mother's lover? My own father? I threw back my head and laughed, my breath exploding in puffs of steam around me. I couldn't even be certain it was I who'd been left with Dr. Avery. My visits to his office seven and eight years later had prompted no sign of recognition on his part, while I, of course, had retained no memory whatsoever of the harrowing episode on his doorstep.

I was pacing up and down in Lara's yard, tripping over an obstacle course of firewood, kindling, and other debris, already cold to the bone in spite of being outside for no more than ten minutes, when something made me stop and turn around. Lara stood looking at me from inside a window on the porch near the front door, her large, flat face expressionless and unreadable in the bright light which surrounded it. She remained motionless, staring in my direction like a figure in a dream. I stamped on the frozen ground and hugged myself in an effort to keep warm. Finally giving up, I turned to go, pausing for a moment to wave goodbye to her, and laughed out loud again. This time I sounded quite crazed, like someone who has just stumbled over hidden treasure, and, in his excitement to possess it, kicks it further and further away.

Breakdown on Broadway

The immense artist Jurgens stayed in his room and sulked.

His "Dance of the Carpenters," a performance art piece in which men and women dressed as river carp boarded Manhattan city buses and confronted passengers with T-squares and hammers, had been a qualified success, to say the least.

He had instructed his actors, whom he preferred calling his collaborators, that mere presentation of the implements of their trade was enough, the heart of the piece being his demonstration of surprise, so that physical confrontation of any kind ran contrary to the concerns of the artist. The carpenter-fish were to restrict their movement to dancing lightly up and down the aisle while displaying the tools of their trade. "Simply pick a passenger and show him your tool," he had instructed. "When the bus has gone six city blocks, pull the cord and leave."

Eight carpenters were chosen from among his acquaintances in SoHo and TriBeCa and it was here, Jurgens felt in retrospect, that he had made his mistake:

they were artists too. Jurgens dressed them in beautiful fish costumes made from thousands of tiny bronzed aluminum disks laboriously sewn together on sturdy burlap frames. Their face masks, spray-painted rose and speckled with gold, had wonderful long whiskers and bulging blue and white eyeballs. Each fish carried a tool, and the selection of the eight tools had been a special source of satisfaction for Jurgens. A hammer, a T-square, a bubble balance, an electric drill, a saw, a coffee can filled with nails, a pair of white canvas work gloves, and a big swatch of kitchen linoleum. He had rented an Econoline van in which he transported the carpenter-fish to the corner of Bleecker and Broadway where they were to catch the downtown bus. It was a bright afternoon and as they alighted from the van their scales glittered in the sun. Each carpenter was given a token.

But no sooner had they filed onto the bus and each selected a passenger—most of whom turned out to be Chinese kitchen workers just off the job, on their way to an annual reunion of Chinese kitchen workers somewhere on Pell Street—than things had started to go wrong. The immense Jurgens wasn't on the bus, of course. He was following it in the rented van, but he learned soon after how his friends had betrayed him.

Apparently the bus driver, a middle-aged black man, had let the carpenters onto the bus without paying the slightest attention to their costumes, indeed without acknowledging them in any way, and the last carp on the bus took it into his head to resent this. As the bus moved back to the traffic on Broadway, the carp leaned over until his whiskers blocked the driver's vision and shouted, "I am a carpenter! This is a tool of my trade!" He waved his swatch of kitchen linoleum in the man's face. The driver, reacting suddenly as if he saw them all for the first time, let out a guttural shout and peremptorily ordered the fish off his bus, simultaneously fending off carp #8 with one arm while trying to steer the bus toward the curb with the other. The carp lost his balance and lurched against the driver as the vehicle shot sideways.

At the very same moment, a taxi which had been behind the bus and had overtaken it on one side, decided to cross in front of it and turn right off Broadway, accelerating steadily as he did so. But the taxi driver swerved back toward the center of the street to avoid a jaywalker who had emerged from between two parked cars. The bus driver slammed on his brakes, but not before he had caught the taxi between his bus and one of the parked cars, narrowing the entire taxi by at least a foot.

Meanwhile, the other carp hadn't been idle. As the bus weaved and lurched to a stop accompanied by the screech of metal being crushed, all of them had lost their balance, tripping over the awkward burlap frames just as they had disengaged their tools from their pockets. The terror-stricken kitchen workers, who a moment before had been sleepily turning the pages of Chinese newspapers, found themselves in the embrace of huge, squirming gold carp which seemed to be attacking them with hammers. One pale overworked cook's assistant went berserk, as he looked up just in time to see a long metal bit from an electric drill pass entirely through his arm and lodge itself in the wall of the bus above his seat. His mouth filled with the taste of burlap and metallic fish scales, and for one terrible moment he thought he was back in the cramped, suffocating hold of the freighter which had smuggled him across the Pacific Ocean some ten months before. Screaming thickly the cook leaped to his feet with eyes starting out of his head and in the process left a good part of his upper arm quivering on the wall. When he turned and saw this, and looked down at the blood racing out of the wound, his shrieks redoubled and he lunged toward the carp sprawled out on the seat, tearing its head off. He then began punching and clawing at that person's face, and finally closed his hands around the throat and spasmodically choked the man to death.

The seven other carp, paralyzed by shock, looked on in horror. As the bus ground to a halt the carp found themselves being beaten with their tools by a dozen angry, fearful Chinese men. Although absorbing most of the blows, the burlap sacks in which the carp were dressed made it impossible to defend themselves. But before they had a chance to escape, the bus driver leaped out the front door, sealing everyone inside before he ran along Broadway in search of a cop.

Several minutes later the policeman, the immense Jurgens, and the bus driver stood on the sidewalk looking through the windows at the pandemonium inside the bus, which resembled an aquarium during a hurricane, with the large delicately colored carp, their whiskers and flanks torn, swooping from side to side in order to avoid the blows of small delirious men dressed in baggy trousers and t-shirts. The cop kept looking up and down the length of the bus, searching for some corner of the action which would make sense. Finally the driver pried the front door open, and as Jurgens started to lift his huge bulk onto the bus, the cop clamped a hand on his shoulder and pulled him back to the sidewalk.

"Where do you fit into this?" he asked.

It was then that Jurgens knew his problems were just beginning. Jumping up and down on the sidewalk not ten feet from them, his cap in his hand, a taxi driver cursed and swore, pointing toward the fender of his demolished heap. The bus driver wrestled the first of the combatants off the bus, a crazed and bloody Chinese man whose frantic contortions it took all three men some minutes to subdue. The immense Jurgens found himself sitting on the man's chest while the policeman and the driver led seven distraught river carp onto the sidewalk. Jurgens looked up at his friends with sad, reproachful eyes and didn't say a word. Another cop arrived, waving his nightstick, but was soon put to work directing traffic.

From out of the manufacturing lofts around them, black and Puerto Rican day workers just getting off their shift poured down into the street. They soon surrounded the city bus, laughing and talking, producing ghetto blasters and cans of soda and beer, wisecracking as the group of fish was lined up against a squad car and handcuffed one by one. The deceased eighth carp lay stiff on the sidewalk before them.

The U.P.S. Man

I live in the mountains west of Boulder, Colorado. The road I live on is called Four Mile Canyon, though actually it winds for five miles, not four, from Boulder Canyon, which is the route from Boulder on the plains to Nederland in the mountains. Four Mile Canyon has houses on the road, houses off the road, and houses hidden in the trees and perched on rocks, near and far, here and there, though on the other hand compared to most of America the road is sparsely populated, and after five miles it ends and you haven't reached my house yet. After five miles Four Mile's asphalt becomes a fork, dirt both ways. I live to the left, one and a half miles further along. That is, after one and a half miles with not a dozen houses, you come to a cluster of cabins called Wallstreet. That's where I live. My neighbors are mostly young people, not mountain people, though there are mountain people here and there, and the young people consider themselves mountain people, though they're not. Many of them aren't young anymore, either, though they're still "young people," and some of them are young people in the process of turning into mountain people by virtue of continuing to be here, though not turning into the mountain people who came before, who were miners and the rest of that—gold miners, silver miners, and saloon-keepers, loggers and blue-eyed lady alcoholics. Many but not all of the people who live here now came recently from places like Massachusetts and Florida. Many but not all commute for a living to Boulder every day. Some few, however, do not seem to do this, despite the system of our times. People live tucked away in these mountains who don't run downtown to work. But they are people one doesn't see much. They keep to themselves, chopping wood, drawing water. Except for the U.P.S. man. The U.P.S. man, if you live where I live in these mountains, you see every day.

I guess I'd been living here for nearly a year before I became aware of something. I'd been a busy and distracted person like everyone else, working in Boulder and not spending day after day up here, but then came the time when I found myself free of the obligation to work in town. Not three weeks passed before I became aware of the U.P.S. man; that is, I had noticed the shiny brown delivery van before, but I had never looked at it. I had never really seen it. One day, as it passed on the road for the hundredth time, I looked up from the book I was reading and a chill went down my spine. I dropped my book and stood up, and soon I was pacing back and forth. I felt nervous and smoked many cigarettes that day. The U.P.S. man shouldn't have been here. There was no way a U.P.S. van could have a daily route on our road. There simply aren't enough people on the road to warrant it. After Wallstreet the road, with few houses on it, climbs into the mountains and turns into a jeep trail. It doesn't go anywhere else. But four or five times a week the U.P.S. van drives up and down the road, usually in the morning, and often the driver stops and parks, or gets out and walks around, looking into a mailbox now and then, smoking a Marlboro. Always he is dressed in the dark brown uniform of the United Parcel Service—a young, athletic-looking man with short blond hair and a blond mustache.

After that day I began to look at the U.P.S. man and his van with interest. Not that I had the opportunity to really study him, because I live on the rare straight stretch of an otherwise winding road, and what traffic there is does roll along. Besides, for a while still I had other things to do. I wasn't going to drop everything for a possible premonition, and so I turned it into a joke, actually. When I get right down to it, a man who for reasons unknown to himself somehow procures a U.P.S. delivery van (a nearly new one, at that) and uniform, or at least a dark-brown flannel shirt and brown pants, and drives up and down our road, day after day—someone like that elicits a nervous kind of laughter. But have I ever so much as checked to see if he wears different pairs of pants of similar color? Have I looked for the famous-make back pocket label that would betray him, since there is no such label on a United Parcel Service uniform? I haven't even inquired of the United Parcel Service company itself: are their men issued uniforms, or are they free to wear anything so long as it's dark brown? How can I say I'm seriously investigating the situation when I haven't asked these questions?

But the fact remains. The fact remains. The guy cruises the neighborhood. He drives back and forth, over a section of road not a mile long, disappearing and then reappearing thirty minutes later, and occasionally an hour after that. I've seen him, as I said, get out and check a mailbox, clipboard in hand, then drive fifty yards up the road to chat with a neighbor. I've never yet seen him on a Saturday or Sunday. But I've never seen him deliver a package, either. And I've never yet seen him on Four Mile Canyon Road itself, which is a mere mile and a half away.

However, the conclusion I'm left with is also a problem. This person is acting out the fantasy of being a U.P.S. man. This person bought the van and acquired the clothing. He decided to face that particular fantasy and make its life his own. Maybe he once worked for the United Parcel Service and things didn't go right for him after that. Maybe he felt he was let go unfairly and is keeping in shape for after a favorable court ruling, when the company will be forced to let him resume his duties. But whatever the explanation, the U.P.S. man doesn't appear furtive or withdrawn. He waves when we pass each other on the road. He waves and smiles. And my neighbors around here, notoriously self-involved people, will be of no help in clearing up this matter. In fact, I once asked my neighbor immediately to the west, the one who makes guitars and mandolins, but whom I often see walking the length of Wallstreet early in the morning, shod always in nylon track shoes no matter what the season, and returning in the afternoon exhausted, his hands black with grease as though he had been installing a transmission, but day after day—I asked that neighbor recently, and he grinned and said, "That's the U.P.S. man, right?" He turned and hobbled back up the snow-covered road to his house, and I returned to sit in the doorway of mine, elbow on my knee and chin sunk into my palm, staring reflectively into the pines. The sky often is bright blue here with no clouds whatsoever, but when the strong wind roars down canyons from the snow peaks of the continental divide, the steep hills catch it and the wind lifts snow into the air, until on some days tidal waves of white powder swirl down the slopes, painting out the sky, the trees, and the houses, and on a day in reality possessed of blue skies and brilliant sunlight I look out my window and can't see anything at all.